# POWDER RIVER

As the State Governor's lawmen spread throughout Wyoming, the days of the bounty hunter are coming to a close. For hired gun Brad Thornton, this spells the end of an era. The men in badges aren't yet everywhere, though, and rancher Moreton Frewen needs immediate action: rustlers are stealing his stock, and Thornton is just the man to make the culprits pay. But these are no run-of-the-mill cattle thieves. The Morgan gang are ruthless killers, prepared to turn their hands to anything from bank robbery to murder . . .

JACK EDWARDES

# POWDER RIVER

*Complete and Unabridged*

**LINFORD**
*Leicester*

First published in Great Britain in 2014 by
Robert Hale Limited
London

First Linford Edition
published 2015
by arrangement with
Robert Hale Limited
London

A catalogue record for this book is available
from the British Library.

ISBN 978–1–4448–2571–8

Published by
F. A. Thorpe (Publishing)
Anstey, Leicestershire

Set by Words & Graphics Ltd.
Anstey, Leicestershire
Printed and bound in Great Britain by
T. J. International Ltd., Padstow, Cornwall

This book is printed on acid-free paper

# 1

'Hold it right there, stranger! Rein in an' keep your hands where I can see 'em!'

Brad Thornton did as he was ordered. He'd seen the rider emerge from the stand of cottonwoods a few moments before and kept his eyes on the old-timer, who was no shootist, that was for sure. By the time he'd reached for the trigger, Thornton reckoned, he could have shot him twice, maybe three times. The old cowboy didn't know it, but he was lucky that Thornton was at Powder River only to talk with his boss.

'State your business, stranger.'

'The name's Thornton. I'm here to see Mr Frewen.'

'Aw, heck, I'll be danged!' The cowboy lowered his long gun and pushed back his hat, showing almost white hair. 'You must reckon us jumpy as a cornered rattler.' He pushed the long gun into its sheath and Thornton saw the cowboy was armed with an old Sharps Army rifle, its barrel held in the stock by three iron bands.

'Glad to meet you, Mr Thornton. We heard lots about you from old friends in Montana. Folks call me Silver cos o' my hair. We wuzn't expectin' you fer another month.'

'Howdy, Silver. I got finished ahead o' time. Took a few days' rest in Cheyenne, been on the trail since.'

'I bin to Cheyenne once. Town's too quiet fer me.' He grinned, showing a toothless mouth. 'Cow towns down in Kansas more to my likin'.' He turned the head of his horse. 'I'll ride up with you to the Big House. Mr Frewen's got one o' them picture-makin' fellers visitin'.' He made a sucking sound with one cheek. 'Last time I saw one of them fellers was at Bull Run, an' Mr Matthew Brady was takin' our pictures before we started gettin' blown to smithereens on Henry Hill.' Silver

2

shrugged. 'But that's fifteen years ago. An' folks don't wanna hear about that any more.'

Thornton didn't reply. Give Silver a chance, he reckoned, and he'd be fighting Johnny Reb until they reached the Frewen house. The two men rode for another half an hour before Thornton saw a large single-storey building set on a slight rise. A cluster of smaller buildings were set to one side and there was a large corral maybe a hundred yards from the front of the building.

Two heavy-looking animals were in the corral, one at each side. As Thornton reached it he could see a line of posts down the centre keeping the animals apart. They were bulls, that was obvious, but of a breed Thornton failed to recognize. Were they from England, maybe? He'd heard that Frewen, who'd come out West for the hunting, had soon learned there was big money to be made out of cattle.

The two men reached a number of

posts stuck in the ground, one of which bore a painted sign announcing the Frewen house. Silver turned his horse.

'I'm gonna leave you here, Mr Thornton. Mr Frewen don't care for the hands getting too close. Jest ride up to the house, an' you'll see a hitchin' post. One of the men workin' fer Mr Frewen will see you comin'.' Silver tugged at the brim of his battered hat. 'When you catch up with them no-goods, watch that rattlesnake Bart Morgan. He's a back-shooter.'

'I'll remember that, Silver.'

Thornton walked his horse towards the house. The late afternoon sun glinted on glass in the windows, whose heavy shutters were pulled back against the wall of the house. Clearly, money had been spent to make the house comfortable for its occupants. Glass windows for a ranch house in the Territory were unusual. They'd help to keep the house warm, especially during the harsh Wyoming winters. Did Frewen and his friends remain here when the heavy snows were

4

falling? He reached the hitching rail Silver had mentioned as the high door at the centre of the building was opened and a tall, thin man stood in the doorway.

'Mr Thornton, I presume, sir,' the man called.

Thornton went up the three steps to the boardwalk, which he guessed ran around the whole of the house.

'My name is Bannock, sir, Mr Frewen's manservant.'

'How did you know I'm Thornton?'

'We have our ways, sir.'

'You're smart, Mr Bannock. I guess Silver gave you the signal.'

Bannock allowed himself a brief smile. 'If you'll follow me, sir, I'll show you through to Mr Frewen's study.'

For a second, Thornton thought himself back to his early days in the Army being shown into the colonel's office by a grizzled sergeant or a young ambitious officer. He followed Bannock twenty paces along a narrow corridor until they reached a solid door bearing a large iron lock. Bannock rapped loudly on the door, and, apparently hearing an invitation to enter, opened it.

'Mr Thornton, sir,' Bannock announced.

A tall, fair-haired man was in the process of moving behind the large mahogany desk and taking his seat. Thornton was surprised to see Frewen dressed in fringed buckskins, and surmised this was the garb the Englishman had chosen to wear for the photographs. Back in England Frewen's friends might think he spent the day chasing Apaches. Thornton bit back a smile. Maybe that's what the Englishman intended. Frewen settled in his own chair, and waved a hand at the chair in front of the desk.

'Come and sit down.' He looked past Thornton towards Bannock. 'I shall need Macrae, but I'll ring when I'm ready.'

'Very well, sir.'

Thornton heard the door close behind him. For the job he'd just finished in Montana he'd been hired in a saloon with a calico queen on the hirer's knee and her arm around his neck. Obviously, this was going to be different.

'Tell me about yourself, Thornton.'

'Not a lot to tell. West Point, Army for five years, then resigned my commission — '

'Why did you do that?' Frewen cut in.

'I got tired of taking orders.'

'And after the Army?'

'Cattle drive on the Texas trail.'

Frewen raised his eyebrows. 'I can't see you as a cowboy.'

'The owner of the beef wanted to take his young son along. My job was to keep the boy alive.' Thornton's mouth twitched at the memory. 'The boy tried hard to get himself killed but I got him home. The boss of the outfit mentioned my name to an English company who'd invested money in Montana. They wanted someone to protect their interests. That's the way I've been working these past five or six years.'

'Unusual work for an educated man.'

Thornton shrugged and remained silent.

'To business, then,' Frewen said. 'I've had too many of my cattle run off for me to ignore the losses any longer. I will not have this ranch made a laughing stock among the cattlemen of Wyoming. You can hang the thieves or shoot them but make sure the word gets around the Territory that anyone who steals again from Powder River will pay the price.'

'Have you reported the rustling to the law?'

'The law's a distant prospect around here. We make our own justice.'

'An' what will you pay me?'

For a moment Frewen appeared taken aback by the bluntness of Thornton's question. 'Four hundred a month and a thousand as a bonus when the job is done.'

'No.'

'I beg your pardon?'

'I get two hundred a week an' two thousand when the job's done. If I don't catch up with the no-goods after three months you don't owe me a penny.'

'But that's nonsense! I'm not going to pay that.'

Thornton stood up. 'Your decision, Mr Frewen. I'll try an' find you a man who'll work for your money. I'd be grateful for a bunk tonight.'

'No, wait!' Frewen's mouth set. 'Sit down, Thornton. Mr Roche told me you were a hard bargainer. I'll pay what you ask. How is Mr Roche, by the way?'

Thornton took his seat again. He'd expected Frewen to put up objections over what he was prepared to pay but he'd been made to look a fool by the rustlers, and no wealthy man, particularly an Englishman, was going to stand for that.

'He's fine,' he said, answering Frewen's question. 'He left for England a coupla months ago. I did a job for a small rancher and then reckoned it was a good time to quit Montana an' look for something different.'

'I'll have your contract put in writing.'

Thornton shook his head. 'There's no need for that. Your word is good enough.' He paused. 'Now tell me what you know about the rustlers.'

'Three Morgan brothers and a black-hearted villain by the name of Darvish. All four are suspected of murder and robbing banks but the law is yet to catch up with them.'

Thornton looked doubtful. 'An' you say they've taken to rustling cattle?'

'Bart Morgan, the eldest brother, has brains. He's a vicious killer but I'm told he's well informed on what goes on in the Territory. He knows he can sell the stolen calves for high prices to the right people.'

'This have something to do with the bulls I saw in the corral?'

Frewen nodded. 'I've successfully crossed Hereford cattle from England with long-horns to produce calves with the toughness of Texans and the generous meat of the Hereford. I'm convinced that one day this cross-breed will be the norm for cattle in this country. Right now, those calves are almost worth their weight in gold.'

Again Thornton looked doubtful. 'I'll not be able to recover the calves.'

Frewen shook his head. 'I shall pursue that problem through the Cattlemen's Association. Your task is to make those villains pay. And I warn you, it will not be easy. The Morgans have a reputation in this part of the Territory. Bart Morgan may not be fully sane and his brother Charlie has a reputation in Colorado as a gunfighter.'

'Any notion where I might make a start?'

Frewen didn't reply directly. Instead, he picked up the small handbell from his desk and rang it vigorously. Immediately, Thornton heard the door behind him open and Bannock's voice.

'Sergeant Macrae, sir.'

Frewen looked over Thornton's shoulder. 'Come in, Macrae. Mr Thornton's arrived to help us with the Morgan brothers.'

Thornton turned to see a man of about fifty years, dressed in a city suit despite the use of his rank. Macrae nodded, his red face bearing an amenable expression.

'I'm pleased to meet you, sir,' he said.

'Ten years ago Sergeant Macrae would have handled the Morgans by himself, but he's far too valuable for me to risk him now,' Frewen said with a smile. 'Tell Mr Thornton what you've discovered, Macrae.'

'It's like this, sir. I've seen two of the Morgan brothers, an' could know 'em agin. I've never laid eyes on Bart Morgan and that other no-good, Darvish, who rides with 'em but Morgan's said to favour a big woollen coat and a blue Dakota hat with a whipped brim. Some folk say he's lost the tip of an ear.'

'That's a good start, Mr Macrae,' Thornton said. 'Have you any notion where we could find 'em?'

'I've heard all four are over at Coyote Bend. It's a settlement a coupla days' ride south. All the no-goods in this part of the Territory are holed up there.'

'Macrae will ride with you to Coyote Bend,' Frewen said. 'You can start tomorrow.'

Thornton shook his head. 'I'll rest up tomorrow. I've been on the trail a long time.'

'Thornton — ' Frewen broke off, apparently having second thoughts about what he was about to say. 'Very well. Bannock will show you where you can sleep.'

Frewen spoke again as Thornton stood up from his chair. 'I wish to make it quite clear that Macrae is riding with you only to identify the Morgans. Sergeant Macrae is a valuable member of my household both here and in England. I do not wish to have him put in danger.'

Thornton glanced at Macrae, who was staring fixedly through the window.

'I understand, Mr Frewen.'

★  ★  ★

Thornton took his breakfast with two of the housemaids, Macrae and the ranch's cook. The cook, whose round figure showed her liking for her dishes, spoke with an accent that baffled Thornton. He assumed she was Scots as she seemed perfectly understood by Macrae. Wherever she came from, she was a good cook and the generous slice of apple pie she'd served Thornton was a welcome alternative to the oats the others were eating. Thornton was tempted to remark that their food was more fit for the horses but decided if he wanted supper he should keep his mouth shut. He finished his coffee, served to him alongside the heavy mugs of tea the others had taken. He stood up from the table.

'I'll ride out and have a word with the range boss, get a feel for what's been going on.'

Macrae nodded. 'Good thinkin', Mr Thornton. You want me along?'

'I'll be OK. I'll be back afore nightfall.'

He left the group at the table and headed out of the ranch building for his horse. Twenty yards from the front of the house Frewen and a young boy were standing together. The Englishman was frowning at what the boy was saying, and as Thornton approached he caught the words.

'But Papa, if I'm to be a rancher I need to see the calves being branded.'

'William, you're not going to be a rancher. You're going to be an important man in England. You may study the Herefords when you return to England. But first you'll learn of serious matters from your new tutor, not about cattle.'

The boy pressed his lips firmly together, frustration showing on his face.

'But Papa — '

'I'm riding out to the brandin',' Thornton said as he approached Frewen and the boy. 'He could ride out with me.'

Frewen spun around. 'It is not your position to speak on this matter, Thornton,' he said brusquely.

Thornton looked at him for a moment. 'You're out West now, Mr Frewen. I'm not one of your servants.'

Frewen's face tightened. For a moment he appeared ready to make some sharp response. Then he relaxed as if reminding himself he was, indeed, no longer in England.

'William, this is Mr Thornton. He's here to help us with the rustlers. Now that I know you have an escort you may ride with him.'

The boy held out his hand, and Thornton, surprised, shook it. 'Good to meet you, William. You get into some other clothes and I'll meet you in the barn.'

Half an hour later when Thornton was wondering how long it took an English boy to change his clothes, William came into the barn. His jacket, made of thick wool, partly covered a woollen shirt. His riding britches and glossy boots made him unmistakeably the son of a wealthy man. Thornton eyed his Mexican spurs.

'You brought those from England?'

'They were here a few days ago hanging on a hook.'

'Those big wheels might look fancy,' he said. 'But they're not kind to the horses.' He walked over to where a pair of Plains spurs hung on the wall of the barn. 'Here, put these on.'

A few minutes later William was examining the saddle on the Appaloosa Thornton had selected, with a doubtful look in his eye. 'The saddle is enormous,' he said. 'It makes me think of one of Mama's chairs.'

Thornton grinned. 'You reckon on bein' a rancher, William, you sit on that for three or four months. You'll be glad it's big.'

'The Appaloosa looks a good horse.'

Thornton raised an eyebrow. He hadn't mentioned the breed of horse.

William took the proffered reins from Thornton, and stepped up lightly, swinging his leg across the Appaloosa. Thornton had to admit to himself that William looked comfortable on a horse, and not the tenderfoot that he'd expected.

They walked their mounts out of the barn and once they were away from the house, urged the animals into a trot and headed south. The late spring morning was clear and there was a hint of summer in the clear sky. Before heading for Wyoming a lawman in Montana had told Thornton there were only three seasons in the Territory — July, August and the rest of the year. The lawman was grinning when he said it, but not that much. Thornton's ride from Cheyenne had been partly across thin snow melting in the warmth of the spring season, but today was pleasant with a weak sun and Thornton was glad of the previous night's rest after weeks on the trail.

For the first half-hour both Thornton and William were silent, each occupied with his own thoughts. Finally, Thornton could remain silent no longer.

'You mind if I say somethin' about your ridin'?'

'What is it, Mr Thornton?'

'I gotta admit you sit as easy on a horse as any cowboy but that eastern style of ridin' ain't gonna go well out here in the West. Daylightin', we call it.'

'In England I've ridden all day without discomfort. Horses don't change because they're in Wyoming.'

'No, but if you mean what you say about ridin' with the men, and your pa gives you the go-ahead, you could be ridin' for a while, not just one day. Mebbe three or four days, mebbe for ten; sometimes fer a whole month.' He saw William hesitate. 'An' risin' in the saddle's gonna make the men laugh, an' you don't want that,' he added.

William frowned and opened his mouth, seemingly intent for a moment on contradicting Thornton. Then he remained silent, watching Thornton carefully. After the two horses had covered maybe another five hundred yards at the trot William reined in to bring the Appaloosa to a walk.

'Very well, Mr Thornton, tell me how.'

'First you gotta sit in the saddle just like it was a comfortable chair, then you gotta push your legs forward.' He watched as William lowered himself into the saddle, adjusting the position of his legs.

'It feels most odd.'

'You'll get used to it. Now hold the reins with just one hand. All the horses out here in the West are neck-reiners. They're trained to turn away from the pressure of the rein.' Thornton watched the boy carefully while the two horses walked along. Pilgrim or not, William appeared to have settled almost immediately.

'OK, see how you feel at the trot.'

William touched his spurs gently on the animal's sides and the Appaloosa broke into a trot. The boy gave a little shout as he thumped on the saddle for a couple of hundred yards, Thornton keeping his roan twenty yards behind him. He didn't expect William to fall off but he guessed he'd be in for a tongue-lashing from Frewen if the boy returned to the ranch house with bruises. Another hundred yards and he saw William had settled to the rhythm of the horse's gait.

'That's fine,' he said, as they both reined in. 'We're gonna lope them now. That's the best speed for coverin' distance when you got a hard ride ahead.'

'Goodness, Mr Thornton! Are you sure I'm ready for this?'

'Don't you worry, William. A lope ain't a gallop. We ain't gonna tire the horses, but a lope's faster than what I reckon you'd call a canter. If you don't care for it, just shout out.'

The boy's mouth set in a firm line. 'Lope away, Mr Thornton!'

Thornton grinned and touched his heels to the sides of his roan. 'I reckon the hands are gonna get themselves a fine cowboy, William!'

★　★　★

They heard the cattle from some distance away. A dust cloud wafted in

21

the blue sky above the animals as they slowly moved across the open land heading for the richer grass. The sagebrush had yet to take a hold as the eight hundred head had been moved as often as necessary to allow the grass to recover. As Thornton and William got closer they could see the fire burning and with the breeze in their faces begin to smell the singed hair and flesh of the calves being branded.

'Lotsa folk don't like the brandin',' warned Thornton as their mounts covered the last hundred yards to where the fire was burning. Around the intense heat of the burning cotton-woods half a dozen men stood, one holding the branding iron as the others wrestled calves to the ground ready for the hot branding iron to be pressed firmly on to the animals' haunches. William wrinkled his nose as the smell of burnt hair became stronger. Thornton saw a rider break away from the bunch around the fire and ride towards them, his hand held high.

'Sorry, folks,' he said, as his mount skittered to a halt. 'We got work here.'

'You the range boss?' Thornton asked.

'That's right. Jack Carling's the name.'

'Brad Thornton, Mr Carling.' He gestured towards William. 'An' this is William Frewen, Mr Frewen's son, fresh out of England.'

Carling looked at the boy, his expression easing. 'Pleased to meet you both,' he said, tugging briefly at the brim of his sweat-stained hat.

'How is the round-up going, Mr Carling?' William asked.

'Better than last spring. We got mebbe four outta five calf crop, and mebbe half of those are bull calves, so we should make some money this fall.' His mouth twisted. 'We'd have made more if it weren't fer those damned rustlers, if you'll excuse my language, Master William.' He stared hard at Thornton, glancing at the Colt on the man's hip. 'I guess you're here to larn 'em that it ain't smart to rustle from Mr Frewen.'

'That's about it, Mr Carling.'

'I got somethin' to show you.' He looked at the boy. 'You wanna take a closer look at the brandin', Master William?'

'Yes, indeed!'

'Then you stay on your horse. There's mother cows around an' they can get a mite ornery when we're handlin' their calves.'

The two men watched William trot the Appaloosa towards the branding before Thornton spoke, a puzzled frown on his face. 'What you got to show me?'

'Mebbe ten minutes away, no more.'

The two men trotted their horses away from where the last few calves were being branded. About a third of a mile away they reined in alongside the animals on the ground. There was the acrid smell of burnt horn and hide lingering in the air. Thornton looked down to see that the animals were unable to stand, their hoofs burnt black.

'I'm damned sure that's Morgan's

work,' Carling said bitterly. 'Stops the mother cows following when the no-goods drive away the calves.'

'How many calves you lost?'

Carling frowned. 'We're still countin'. Mr Frewen's mighty angry that some no-good thinks he can come along an' steal.' He looked up at Thornton. 'You reckon you can chase 'em down?'

'I hear Morgan could be in Coyote Bend with his kin.'

'You watch yourself you come up agin 'em. The Morgan brothers are real bad. Bart's a back-shooter, Charlie and Moses are said to be gun-crazy and Jack Darvish, who rides with 'em, is said to be handy with a gun.'

'You tellin' me four men ran off your cattle?'

'I reckon they had some dumb cowboys with 'em. There's more cowboys than work in these parts fer a coupla months an' some of 'em ain't too fussy how they get their grubstake. They ain't worth you botherin' with 'em. They find work an' they'll be honest men.'

'What d'you know of Coyote Bend?'

'Nothin', an' that's the way it's gonna stay. All the no-goods in the Territory in these parts are holed up there.'

They turned their horses and trotted back to where the cowboys were intent on branding the remaining calves. Suddenly Thornton stood up in his stirrups.

'What the hell . . . ?'

Struggling through the outer growth of a thicket, William, a triumphant smile on his face, was carrying a calf in his arms, unaware of the intent gaze of the mother cow maybe a hundred yards away. A bellow of pure rage echoed around the thicket as the animal dropped its head and began to trot towards the boy.

'Damned young fool!' Thorton swore.

He dug his heels into the sides of his horse, as William, realizing the threat from the mother cow, dropped the calf and began to run for his Appaloosa some fifty yards away. He was never going to make it.

Thornton, crouched low in his

saddle, spurred his horse to greater speed. He was maybe five yards ahead of the mother cow, the animal intent on charging directly at the boy. Thornton leaned away from his saddle, bunched his arm muscles and, as he reached William, heaved the boy up and on to the saddle before him. A frustrated mother cow came to a skidding halt, glaring in the direction of the retreating Thornton. The boy's face, white with shock, his eyes wide, was only a foot or so away from Thornton's.

'I should give you a good slapping,' Thornton snapped.

The boy, held tightly by Thornton, struggled to speak. 'The-the calf was stuck in the thicket and crying. I thought . . . ' His voice trailed away.

Thornton's mount reached the Appaloosa, loosely secured to a low bush and nibbling at the bunch and buffalo grass. He let go of the boy, who slid to the ground.

'Now get on that damned horse and stay there! You've learned two lessons today, William,' Thornton said brusquely, glaring at the boy, his face set. 'First, on the range you do as the range boss tells you. Second, you stay on your horse, an' the beef will respect you. They catch you afoot an' they ain't so friendly.'

Up on his Appaloosa, William looked across at Thornton. 'Are you going to tell my father what happened?'

Thornton shook his head. 'I'll speak with Carling, an' make sure the men keep their mouths shut.' His face relaxed. 'After all, cowboys have to stick together.'

# 2

Thornton and Macrae reined in on the crest of a hill and looked down on the scattering of ramshackle cabins and tents, which stood maybe five hundred yards from a river. Macrae pointed a gnarled finger.

'That's the devil's cauldron they call Coyote Bend,' he rasped. 'Every murderer, bank robber and whoremonger in this part of the Territory finds a place to hide. The sheriff's a drunk an' can be bought for a few dollars. The mayor, cos that's what he calls himself, is said to have rode with Quantrell an' his cut-throats. The only decent man I met was a German who runs the livery stable.'

'We gonna run into trouble when we ride in?'

Macrae shook his head. 'No-goods are comin' in an' out all the time.'

Thornton eased his legs as he took in the view. 'Is that the saloon? The big place in the centre?'

'That's it.' Macrae screwed up his mouth. 'I've drunk their whiskey. It's an insult to the finest drink the Good Lord gave to mankind.'

Thornton grinned. He'd heard lots of stories about the famous whiskey from the Scotsmen in his regiment. He looked up at the sky. 'Night will be on us by the time we reach the town. Is there a boarding house?'

'There's a couple. I tried them both. Neither is a place I'd be willing to lay my head agin. The bugs are as big as jack-rabbits.'

Thornton looked around him. He raised an arm to point in the direction of a stand of cottonwoods to the east of the settlement. 'OK. We could be here for a while. If we need time to track down the Morgans we'll ride outta town an' spend the nights among those trees. Any rider around these parts will be makin' for Coyote so we ain't gonna be disturbed. You OK with that?'

'That'll be fine. I kinda like sleepin' 'neath the stars.' Macrae chuckled. 'Reminds me of ol' times.'

Daylight was fading rapidly by the time Thornton and Macrae reached the muddy gap between the two lines of shacks and tents. Main Street, Coyote Bend, Thornton reckoned, needed some attention. The two men walked their horses, heading for the livery stable. Coyote Bend was the wrong place to leave good animals unattended.

They passed the saloon, the lights from oil lamps throwing a splash of yellow light across the mud of the street. Through the open doorway came the sounds of loud voices, the screeching laughter of women, and beneath the tide of sound Thornton could hear a fiddle being played. With Macrae leading, they reached a shack at the corner of an alleyway near the bathhouse, which bore a fingerpost showing the way to the livery stable. The two men walked their horses down the fifty yards of an alleyway where light was showing from the wide entrance to the livery. Thornton stepped down from his saddle, followed by Macrae.

'Hermann!' Macrae called. 'You around?'

A few moments passed before a small man with bandy legs appeared from behind a wooden board, halfway down the barn. 'Hermann is here,' he called. He brushed at the front of his dark-blue Levis and Thornton guessed the German had been eating supper.

'OK we leave the horses with you for a few hours?'

'Sure, cost you a dollar each.'

Thornton raised his eyebrows. 'You don't come cheap.'

The little man shrugged. 'Plenty of places 'round here to leave good horses. I ain't sure if you — '

Thornton held up a hand. 'OK, two dollars it is. We'll be back in a coupla hours.'

'I ain't goin' no place.'

Ten minutes later Thornton and Macrae stepped into the smoke-laden saloon. The fiddler had ceased playing and was sitting with two other men, his fiddle on the table beside him. Card players sat at half a dozen tables, behind which a heavily set man sat on a high chair, a scattergun across his knees. Sitting with the men at tables were women, some young, some not so young, dressed in cheap, highly coloured shifts, showing plenty of flesh. A heavily powdered woman sat in a corner, her eyes like black pebbles, watching over the women.

Thornton and Macrae reached the bar, finding a gap among the line of men. Macrae called out to attract the attention of the sallow-faced barkeep.

'What's it to be, gents?'

'Two beers,' Thornton said.

'You want the whiskey up front?'

'Just the beers.'

While waiting for the beers the two men turned to survey the crowd before them. Macrae suddenly stiffened. 'I see 'em,' he said quietly. 'Two fellers playin' cards back o' where the fiddler's sittin'.'

Thornton turned back to the bar to

drop a coin on the bar as the barkeep put down the two beers. 'I ain't seen you afore,' the barkeep said. 'You gonna be here a while?'

'Just lyin' low for a few days, then we'll be movin' on.'

'Any special place?'

Thornton stared hard at him, and the barkeep shrugged.

'Just askin',' he said.

Without a further word he moved along the bar to serve another customer, who was banging his pot on the counter to attract attention. Thornton turned back to survey the crowd, his casual look-around giving the appearance of idle curiosity. His gaze finally rested on the two men pointed out by Macrae.

'Who are they?'

'Two of the Morgan brothers. Charlie on the left, Moses on the right. Bart Morgan and Jack Darvish ain't gonna be far away.'

Thornton thought for a moment. Before he made any move he had to wait until Bart Morgan and Darvish appeared. If he were to catch up with all four he needed to be able to recognize them. Then he'd have to work out how to split them up. Even if they weren't as tough as folks said, taking on four together would only gain him a one-way ticket to Boot Hill.

He saw three men get up from a table, leaving their cards among bottles and glasses. 'We'll grab that table,' he said to Macrae. 'How's your cards?'

Two hours later Thornton was still dealing cards across the table to Macrae, who proved to be a better player than he'd claimed. Thornton was grateful that they weren't playing for real money or he'd have been into Macrae for a heap of cash. He was looking down at his cards when Macrae laid down his own cards with a flourish and a large grin on his fleshy face. Four kings showed their faces to Thornton, who put down his cards with a resigned shake of his head.

'That's a half a million you owe me,'

Macrae said. The grin disappeared and he glanced across at the two Morgan brothers, who still sat at their table, drinking whiskey and playing cards. 'You reckon we're gonna see Bart Morgan an' Darvish?'

Thornton shook his head. 'Time we headed out to the cottonwoods.' He drank the final inch of his beer and stood up. 'We could be here for a few days.'

The two men made their way out of the saloon and along the boardwalk to the alleyway leading to the livery. There'd been rain while they were in the saloon and boards had been placed in the centre of the alleyway to provide a clear path over the mud to the livery. They stepped off the final board and into the yellow light thrown by the oil lamps. The little German came out to the middle of the barn to meet them.

'Howdy, gents, your hosses are right there.' He pointed to two stalls halfway down the barn. 'Fed an' watered. I took a look at their plates but they're fine.

You'll find everythin' OK.'

'Thanks, Hermann. We'll be back tomorrow. Any place we can get breakfast?'

'We got our own Chinaman just along from the saloon. Food's OK but his coffee ain't up to much.'

'We'll see you tomorrow.'

Thornton was leading his horse to the centre of the barn when a thought came to him. 'Hermann, you know the Morgan brothers?'

'Sure. They keep their mounts here.'

'An' Darvish, who rides with 'em?'

'Him as well. Bart Morgan an' Jack Darvish rode out a coupla days ago. Said they had business and might not be back for a while.'

'You know where they're goin'?'

Hermann shook his head. 'They don't say an' I don't ask.'

'Two Morgan brothers were in the saloon tonight.'

'Wettin' their whistles afore a hard ride, I reckon,' Hermann said. 'They're ridin' out at first light tomorrow.'

37

Thornton handed the reins of his roan to the German. 'Put him back in the stall. I'm gonna have a word with Mr Macrae.' He walked down the barn followed by Macrae, a puzzled frown on the old sergeant's face. Out of earshot of the German, Thornton turned to him.

'I'm stayin' here and takin' the Morgans when they come in tomorrow. You ride out to the cottonwoods an' I'll catch up with you.'

'One against two? These Morgans ain't penny-ante thieves,' Macrae said. 'They're fast an' they're killers.'

'OK, but I've got surprise on my side. They're not expectin' trouble comin' in here.'

Macrae's face hardened. 'You're gonna get yourself killed you take 'em on alone. I'm gonna stand with you.'

Thornton breathed in deeply. He'd expected Macrae to put up objections but Frewen had given him his instructions. Macrae was along only to help identify the Morgans, not to involve himself in a gunfight with no-goods who, in Macrae's own words, were fast and wouldn't hesitate to kill.

'Sergeant Macrae,' he said evenly, 'Moreton Frewen put me in charge, that's why he's payin' me. So I'm givin' you a lawful order. Ride out to the cottonwoods and wait for me to join you.'

Macrae was silent for a few moments, and then his lips pulled back in a wry expression. 'I shoulda guessed you were Army.'

Thornton shrugged. 'Some while back.'

'You don't show an' I'm gonna come back.'

Thornton nodded. 'OK. But wait a day. If I'm not back by then, you ride to Powder River an' explain what's happened. Tell Frewen he needs to hire a new man.'

Macrae held out his hand. 'Best o' luck, Major.'

Thornton grinned. 'Never made more than captain, Mr Macrae.'

He watched Macrae ride clear of the barn and turned back to the German, who was waiting halfway along the stables. From an inside pocket of his trail coat he pulled two coins and held them so Hermann could see their value.

'I stay here overnight, Hermann.'

The German glanced down at the coins. 'You gonna kill those two Morgans when they show?'

'Not unless I have to.'

'You can't leave one here alive. He'll kill me for sure.'

'I know that. Both go with me alive or dead.'

'S'posin' you ain't as fast with that Colt o' yourn as you think you are?'

'Then you got some fast talkin' to do.'

The German looked down again at the coins in Thornton's outstretched hand. 'A dead 'un I can handle. It's one left alive an' free that scares me.'

'I'll see to it,' promised Thornton. 'You got anywhere I can sleep for a coupla hours?'

Hermann pointed at the board from

which he'd appeared previously. 'There's a bunk behind there,' he said. 'It ain't grand, but there's a coupla blankets.'

Thornton handed him the money. 'You cross me, Hermann, and Macrae will be back to settle accounts.'

'I ain't gonna cross you. For this money you can come and kill as many of those no-goods as you've a fancy to.'

★　★　★

After the previous day's hard riding Thornton had slept longer than he'd intended but a couple of hours before daybreak he'd been awake and drinking the hot coffee the German had produced for him.

'The money you're payin' I reckoned you deserve a little hotel service,' Hermann had said. 'An' if it's the last coffee you drink in this world you cain't say it ain't good.'

Now, as the darkness of the night outside the barn began to turn to grey, Thornton was standing a few feet from

41

the entrance, leaning against the wooden wall. He was gambling that the Morgans would step into the barn on the side he was standing. Should they come in from the other side, out of his reach, he'd have to think again.

He'd have liked a smoke but the German said he didn't allow smoking in the barn no matter how much he got paid. Thornton couldn't help smiling at the German's insistence on proper safety measures when his livery was in a place like Coyote Bend. Looking after the no-goods' horses so efficiently, Thornton guessed, was what kept Hermann out of trouble.

The little German came over as being a decent man, although what he was doing in Coyote was a mystery. Thornton was trying to guess at possible explanations when he heard voices. Two men were in conversation, their boots sounding on the boards across the mud, their spurs jingling. The Morgans, maybe? Then he caught the word 'Bart', and knew the time had come.

He sucked in air, drew his Navy Colt and held it loosely down by his side, tensing the muscles in his arm. The voices neared the entrance to the barn, and he was amazed to see Hermann appear from behind the board and walk towards the entrance.

'Howdy, gents. Looks to be a fine day for a ride. Gotya hosses right here.'

Two men stepped into the barn, the light falling on their features showing Thornton they were the two men identified by Macrae the previous evening. He took one pace out of the shadows and lashed at the side of the leading man's head with the barrel of his Colt. There was the crunch of bone and Charlie Morgan went down like a falling tree. A cry of fury erupted from Moses Morgan close behind. He whirled towards Thornton, his sidearm already inches out of its holster.

Thornton shot him once, the heavy slug smashing into the centre of the man's body. Moses staggered a couple of feet, blood spurting from his chest, and went down amongst the straw at the entrance to the barn. Thornton took two paces forward, bent down to thrust the barrel of his Colt against the man's forehead and pulled the trigger. Bone fragments flew through the air and grey matter splattered against the side of the barn.

'Jesus Christ!' The German, his eyes wide with shock, his jaw slack, stared mesmerized at the dead Morgan brother. 'You play goddamned rough, mister.'

'Get me a length of rope so I can hog-tie this no-good afore he comes 'round,' Thornton ordered.

'Sure, sure! Right away!'

Once again Hermann disappeared behind the board to emerge a few moments later carrying a length of rope. In his other hand he carried a glass flask.

'Here,' he said, calmer now. 'This'll straighten you out. You ain't so easy as you're makin' out.'

Thornton took the flask. 'When I get used to killing I'll find other work.'

He took a long gulp from the flask,

feeling the powerful spirit running down his insides and burning away the reaction to what he'd just done. He'd never found it easy to take another man's life and it was getting harder. He lowered the flask and wiped his mouth with the back of his hand.

'That's damned good stuff.'

'Schnapps from the old country,' Hermann said, taking a pull on the flask himself.

Thornton took the rope from Hermann and dropped to one knee to lash the hands of the unconscious Charlie Morgan.

'The shootin' gonna bring folks here?' Thornton asked.

Hermann shook his head. 'Not in this place. Folks stay clear of shootin' unless they're doin' it themselves.'

'I'll help you clean up.'

Again the German shook his head. 'I'll give you a hand to get Charlie across his horse. Then you ride outta here.'

Thornton nodded in the direction of

the dead man. 'What about him?'

'You leave Moses to me. An' you don't need to ask questions. I got his horse an' his rig. That'll square us.'

Both men heaved the roped Morgan, still unconscious, across his horse, and Hermann rigged the horse on a long lead rein and secured it to the horn of Thornton's saddle. Thornton led the two horses to the doorway of the barn, and mounted his own horse. He looked down at the little German.

'Why the hell don't you get outta this place?'

Hermann was silent for a few moments as if considering whether to ignore the question, and then he looked up directly at Thornton. 'I bin with the same woman here for ten years,' he said slowly. 'The doc says she'll be dead in six months.' His mouth twisted. 'Then I'll move on.'

Thornton nodded, and touched the brim of his hat. 'Mebbe I'll see you around. Buy her somethin' fancy with the money I gave you.'

'I'll do that.'

Thornton turned the head of his mount and rode out into the early light.

# 3

Brad Thornton was five hundred yards from the main street of Alveston when he reined in his horse and leaned back in the saddle. He slipped his boots from his Plains stirrups and stretched, easing the stiffness in his leg muscles. He was beginning to weary of the long days in the saddle and sleeping under the stars.

Maybe he should call it a day and go back East, take it easy for a while. He had enough money in the bank to do as he pleased for a year or more. But first he had to catch up with Bart Morgan and Jack Darvish. He'd made a deal with the Englishman Frewen and the money he'd agreed to pay was too much to ignore.

But he had to admit the hunt for the no-goods was proving to be tough. In the month since he'd left Powder River he'd been in more saloons, drunk more rot gut whiskey and played more poker with both honest men and no-goods than at any time in the previous five years.

Morgan and Darvish could be in no doubt now that they were being trailed. Thornton had expected them to split up but in the last town he'd rested his horse he'd had reliable information that the two men were sticking together. Maybe they were reckoning that if it came to a gunfight two men were better than one. But why would they run to a town like Alveston? Sure, there was a bank, a big one, and plenty of money in the town brought in by the railroad and from the ranches. But folks had told him there were also two deputies, a tough sheriff by the name of Landon and a bunch of Volunteers, all ex-soldiers.

For a few seconds he blew air through pursed lips, thinking over what he should do. First, he had to change his horse. His roan had broken a leg in a jack rabbit hole and shooting the animal was something he could have done without. The only horse he'd been able to buy from a coach station was too small. Once he'd attended to business at the livery he'd take a beer in the saloon and wash the trail dust from his mouth. Men like Morgan and Darvish would always drift into a saloon and maybe someone there would remember them. He settled his gunbelt and touched his heels to the sides of his mount.

Alveston was a busy town. Men and women thronged the boardwalks in front of the stores; wagons rattled to and fro along Main Street; drummers stepped smartly between the stores, carrying their bags of samples. Many of the men were in working clothes, while a few sported city suits and derby hats. Most of the women wore simple cotton dresses, some with shawls around their shoulders against the cool breeze of early spring.

Fashionable women, followed closely by young girls carrying their parcels, wore smart dresses, button shoes showing beneath their skirts as they walked briskly along the boardwalks, intent on their errands. With so many women around it was apparent that Alveston had been settled for several years.

The boards outside the stores offered the townsfolk a variety of goods, likely to have been brought to the town by the railroad spur, which lay to the east of Main Street. Thornton guessed that the town was a trading centre for this corner of Wyoming Territory.

He rode past the sheriff's office, its door ajar as if waiting for business. If either Morgan or Darvish were hereabouts, the sheriff was going to be busier today than maybe he expected. Fifty yards down the street a brightly painted board announced the Silver Horse saloon. Although it was early in the day, the place appeared to be open for business. Thornton saw a tall, heavily set man step through the batwing doors and disappear from view.

A livery sign bore a roughly painted arrow that pointed down an alley. Thornton walked his mount off Main

Street and stepped down from his saddle as he turned into the alley. He walked the ten yards to the big open doors of the livery, his hand grasping the reins of his mount. As he stepped into the barn he breathed in the sweet tang of oats, hay and horses. The livery was neat and tidy and he knew the animals would be well looked after.

A man in blue coveralls, a woollen hat on his head, appeared from out of one of the stalls. 'Howdy, stranger. The name's Butler. How can I help?'

'Howdy, I'm Thornton.' He frowned. 'What's that you're holdin'?'

Butler grinned and held up a straight length of wood bearing feathers at one end. 'An Injun arrow. I gotta Shoshone workin' for me, so I'm tryin' my hand. It takes a whole day's work to make a good arrow.' He shrugged. 'Anyways, what can I do fer you?'

'I need a bigger horse, a good one. This one's OK but she's a mite small for me.'

Butler took a calculated look at

Thornton and then moved to stand by the horse. 'Yeah, see what you mean. I reckon we can fix something. I'm looking for a mare this size, and I've a big roan in the corral at the end of town. You wanna ride down there an' take a look?'

'Sounds good to me.'

Back in the street, as he stepped up to his saddle, Thornton could feel the morning sun chasing away the breeze and warming his back. The soft dirt of Main Street was giving way to hardpack as the moisture remaining from the melted snow dried out. He looked around, recalling he'd seen no sign of a corral. He needed the other end of town. He turned his mount's head and walked her down the street. A couple of cowboys, one riding a grulla, half-nodded to him as he passed.

He covered maybe three hundred yards, the boardwalks coming to an end with a bathhouse on one side of Main Street opposite a place announcing that billiards could be played for five cents.

Main Street gave way to the trail leading south.

Fifty yards on, a small corral, its painted posts gleaming white, was occupied by a single horse. The animal raised its head as Thornton's mount approached the corral but after a moment went back to nibbling at the grass. Thornton stepped down from the saddle, looped the reins over a bar and clambered over the top rail and into the corral.

He walked up to the big roan, keeping a close eye on the animal. Butler hadn't said the animal was ornery but if he was trying for a sale then maybe he thought it not worth mentioning. The last thing Thornton wanted was a kicking.

He was being over-cautious, he decided a moment later. The roan raised its head and nuzzled Thornton's cupped hand, picking up his scent. Thornton stroked the side of the animal's neck for a moment and the animal turned soft brown eyes in his direction as if in appreciation of

Thornton's good manners.

'Thornton, you sonovabitch! Turn 'round cos I ain't a back-shooter!'

For a second Thornton felt the muscles clench across his gut. Then he stepped away from the horse, turning slowly to look across the corral at the man who stood maybe twenty feet away. Tall, thick-set, and with a short beard, the man was dressed from head to foot in black.

Who the hell was he? This wasn't Bart Morgan. The man's face above the beard was unmarked and he remembered that Morgan was missing part of his ear. So was this stranger someone he'd crossed over the last couple of years and was now keen to get his revenge? He didn't have long to wait to find out.

'We bin lookin' fer you, Thornton. Bart's gonna be real pleased that I caught up with you.'

The threatening stranger had to be Jack Darvish. The warning he'd been given at Powder River came back to him. Darvish was fast and wouldn't hesitate to shoot. But could he shoot straight? A hot tingling at the back of his neck told him he was about to find out.

'Darvish! You ride with Morgan, an' you're gonna be swinging from a rope. The Englishman is righteous. You'll do time in Cheyenne but you'll be alive.'

Moving slowly across the corral as he spoke, Thornton came to a halt when he judged he was maybe thirty feet from Darvish. He hadn't yet come up against any no-good who could hit his target at that distance and he was banking on Darvish being no different.

'Walk down the street with me, an' we'll talk with the sheriff. He's said to be an honest man who follows the law.'

'You're goddamned crazy!'

Darvish's hand dropped to his sidearm. An instant later Thornton heard the smash of the slug into the rail somewhere behind him as the sound of the shot reached him. The roan went skittering across to the other side of the corral. A second shot from Darvish kicked up dirt a foot away from Thornton's boot.

Draw. Aim. Breathe in. Fire.

The heavy slug from Thornton's Navy Colt hit Darvish an inch above his heart. He was probably dead before his body hit the ground. But it was wise to always make sure. Thornton walked steadily across the corral, his Colt aimed at the body. Darvish lay on his back, his open eyes staring sightlessly at the sky. Thornton kicked away the fancy Smith & Wesson, and squatted to search the man's pockets.

'Hold it right there, stranger! Put that cannon o' yourn on the ground. Stand up an' face this way. Keep your hands where I can see 'em. An' do it all real slow or the deputy's gonna shoot you down.'

For Christ's sake! Whoever it was who'd called out had been damned quick. He supposed it was the town's sheriff. Thornton remained very still. He'd expected something like this but not so fast. He knew there was no way a stranger could ride into town, get himself into a gunfight and not expect to be challenged by the local law. Moving very slowly, Thornton lowered his Navy the few inches to the loose soil of the corral. He stood up and turned slowly. Outside the corral stood two men, badges pinned to their leather vests. One of them held a Winchester rifle pointing at Thornton. The older man, clearly the sheriff, held his sidearm loosely down by his side.

'He was a cattle-thief,' Thornton called. 'I got hired to track him down.'

'Mebbe so. But we don't take kindly to shoot-outs in this town.'

'His name's Darvish, an' he tried to gun me down.'

'We can talk about that.'

Beyond the sheriff a large crowd had gathered, excited voices calling out questions to the sheriff, who ignored them. Instead, he pointed at the body and gave orders to his deputy.

'Pick up the stranger's gun an' then

get rid o' that body.' He turned to face Thornton. 'You're walkin' down to my place. I'll hear what you gotta say down there.'

Thornton watched as the deputy lowered his Winchester and walked around the edge of the corral and pushed open the gate. He crossed to where Thornton had dropped his Navy, picked it up and then went back to hand the sidearm across the rail to the sheriff.

'My horse is over there,' Thornton said, pointing.

The sheriff turned to the crowd of townspeople, apparently searching for someone. 'Frank Butler, you take care o' the two horses.'

'Sure thing, Mr Landon, I'll have 'em over at the livery.'

Sheriff Landon turned back to Thornton. 'You ain't gonna give me trouble, are you?'

Thornton shook his head. 'No trouble, Sheriff.'

He walked to the gate of the corral and pushed through to Landon, who had moved to join him. Landon turned to the crowd.

'OK, folks. Go about your business unless you fancy joining the stranger down at my place.'

The townsfolk must have known the sheriff meant what he said for within seconds they were heading back towards Main Street, the voices of the women rippling through the clear air like a chattering of small birds. It was obvious to Thornton from the reaction of the townsfolk that a gunfight in the middle of town was a rare event.

'You gotta name, stranger?'

'Thornton. I don't go fer being afoot. We can ride to your place.'

Sheriff Landon's mouth twitched. 'I did that once. No-good took off like a jackrabbit. Took me a whole day to catch up with him. We're gonna walk. Butler will take care of your horse and rig.'

Thornton shrugged. 'Guess I'm lucky to be walkin'.'

Five minutes later he pushed through the open door of the sheriff's office,

Landon close behind him. The sheriff pointed to the chair in front of his desk, and walked behind the desk to take his own chair while Thornton sat down.

Landon pulled a sheet of paper towards him, and took a pen from the inkwell at the edge of his desk. Thornton felt easier. A sheriff who obeyed the niceties of the law was unlikely to railroad him into any hanging party.

'Name agin?'

'Thornton. You wanna hear what the shooting was all about?'

'Go ahead.'

Thornton explained his hunt for the rustlers of the Powder River cattle. How he'd learned that Morgan and Darvish were heading for Alveston and followed them. He was at the business of buying a horse when Darvish had surprised him at the corral.

Landon stared hard at Thornton. 'I ain't got much time for bounty hunters.'

Thornton shook his head. 'I'm no bounty hunter. Like I told you I'm hired to do a job for Mr Moreton

Frewen, who ranches at Powder River. There was no paper on any of Morgan's no-goods in Wyoming. The whole passel came up from some place in Colorado.'

Landon wrote a few words on the paper before him. 'S'posin' I believe all that, you still shot a man down in this town. The councilmen are gonna be askin' me questions.'

'Landon, I was gonna bring him in. Darvish took two shots at me afore I drew my Colt.'

'You askin' me to believe you just stood there, gettin' shot at?'

'That's the way it happened but I wasn't gonna risk him tryin' agin.'

The sheriff shrugged. 'Circuit Judge Harris will decide. He'll be here in a coupla weeks.'

'Fer Chris'sakes, Landon! I can't wait around here. Where would I stay?'

Landon shot him a puzzled stare. 'Where the hell d'you think? You're gonna be in my jail, back o' this place.'

# 4

Thornton sat on the side of his bunk in one of the two cages in the jailhouse, his head bent over his book. He was the only prisoner there and save for several birds exercising their lungs a few yards from the barred window the jailhouse was quiet. That suited him fine. At least he had peace and quiet to finish his reading.

The one-eyed old man, Joe something or other, who did chores for the sheriff, had escorted him out to the privy in the back yard shortly after dawn. A deputy had brought him a bowl of cold water to wash away the night's sleep, and then back in his cell there'd been a plate of beans, a hunk of bread and a mug of coffee brought to him by Joe. When Landon had appeared later Thornton had asked if he could use the town's bathhouse to wash off the trail dust from the previous three weeks and had been told that the sheriff would think about it.

Now he looked up from his book as he heard the door open at the end of the passage and Joe appeared carrying a bunch of keys. Thornton rested his book on one knee while he watched the jailer unlock the door to the cage and step back.

'Sheriff wants to talk,' Joe said. He pulled open the door. 'Don't take too long,' he called over his shoulder as he went back down the passage.

Thornton stood up. Had the judge arrived in town earlier than expected? He picked up his trail jacket from the bunk and shoved his book into one of the broad pockets. He stepped through the door, and went down the passage to enter the sheriff's office.

Landon was in his usual chair behind the desk. In front of him Thornton's gunbelt and Navy Colt rested on a copy of the town's newspaper. In the corner of the office sat an elderly man, a silver-topped cane between his knees. He wore a black city suit, a silk shirt and blue cravat showing beneath the tightly buttoned jacket. On a small table beside him sat a billycock hat.

'Take a seat, Thornton.' Landon waved in the direction of the chair where Thornton had sat the previous day. 'This here gentleman is Mr Warren Jenkins. I'm thinkin' you're a lucky man, cos of him.'

'Then I'm obliged to you, sir,' Thornton addressed the elderly man, 'if it means that I'm outta jail.'

Jenkins nodded. 'I was in my buggy by the trees close to the corral. I saw what happened yesterday when that man threatened you.'

'Then you know what I told you was straight, Sheriff,' Thornton said.

'Your luck's runnin', Thornton,' Landon cut in. 'Tell him the rest, Mr Jenkins.'

'I own the biggest stage line here-abouts, Mr Thornton,' Jenkins said. 'A month ago I was in Cheyenne where I met Mr Moreton Frewen. He explained

65

that he was losing cattle and had hired a good man by the name of Thornton to chase down the rustlers.'

Thornton blew a sigh of relief between pursed lips. 'Mr Jenkins, you sure have been in the right place for me.'

Landon crumpled paper into a ball and tossed it into a bin beside his desk. Then he shoved Thornton's Navy Colt across the desk. 'You're free to go, Thornton. Try not to fire that cannon afore you leave town.' He stared hard across the desk. 'You are leavin' town, I s'pose?'

'If Morgan's still around I'm gonna stay, an' I'll let you know.' Thornton picked up his gunbelt, buckled it around his waist and eased his Colt back into its holster.

'Then don't go havin' gunfights on Main Street or a good word ain't gonna keep you out of jail another time.'

Thornton's mouth twitched. Did Landon ever relax? He turned to the stage-owner. 'Mr Jenkins, can I buy you coffee, or something stronger if you wish?'

'I stopped going into saloons afore nightfall about twenty years ago, Mr Thornton, but I take my coffee in the Majestic about this time. I'll walk across with you.'

Twenty minutes later the two men were alone in the small parlour of the town's hotel. Steam rose from the spout of a tall metal coffee pot and before each man was a thick china cup standing in a saucer.

'I was fortunate you were around, Mr Jenkins.'

Jenkins nodded. 'Two more days and I would have left on the Union Pacific for South Pass City,' Jenkins said. 'I'm travelling with others to an important meeting with Esther Hobart Morris.'

'A woman?'

'No ordinary woman, Mr Thornton. She's the first Justice of the Peace in the Territory, maybe the first in the whole country. Women here have the vote; the law was passed back in sixty-nine.'

'I heard about that. I reckon it's mighty unusual.'

'Do I surmise you're a newcomer to Wyoming?'

'I've been here a while but I was born in Massachusetts, ridden plenty of new trails since then.'

'But why Wyoming?'

'The English have a long reach, Mr Jenkins. I'd been workin' for an Englishman, name o' Roche, when Mr Frewen needed some help with rustlers.' Thornton grinned. 'The English know how to pay a man, so I rode to Powder River beginning of summer.'

'Do you intend to stay there?'

Thornton shook his head. 'One o' these days I'm goin' back East. I'll read the great books, listen to fine music, mebbe even travel to Europe.' He gave an awkward smile, seemingly embarrassed by his admission of his hopes for the future, and keen to change the subject. 'You think the stage business will survive now the railroad's here?'

'I'll be gone afore that happens. But

you're right, Mr Thornton. The days of the Concord coach are coming to an end. There's even talk back East of some machine that will replace the horse. The West is going to see some mighty big changes over the years.' Jenkins took a heavy gold watch from his vest pocket and checked the time. 'Now you must excuse me. I've business to attend today afore I leave.'

The two men stood up and left the hotel together. 'If I can ever be of service to you, Mr Jenkins, an' I'm in the Territory, you only have to ask,' Thornton said, as the two men shook hands before parting.

Thornton stood on the boardwalk, looking up and down Main Street. Nothing had changed from the day before. Why should it? He was just another stranger who'd ridden into town and ended up in jail.

Townsfolk bustled around, probably the same women in workaday cotton dresses with shawls thrown across their shoulders he'd seen the previous day.

Men in blue-bib coveralls went about their business, or stopped to exchange words with their neighbours. Three cowboys rode down the street, calling out to the blacksmith, who was stoking his fire, a horseshoe clenched in giant pincers in his free hand. Thirty yards beyond the forge, the sign showed the Silver Horse. A good place to start, Thornton decided.

He crossed Main Street, quickening his pace halfway across, as a wagon came down the street pulled by a lively-looking animal, which appeared intent on knocking down as many of the townsfolk as it could achieve.

'Mighty sorry, folks,' the driver shouted. 'Betsy got her tail up this mornin'.'

Thornton stepped up to the board-walk and pushed through the batwing doors. The place was certainly different from the honky-tonks he'd been into during the previous weeks. The solid wooden bar, which might have been built from mahogany, and the large mirror pinned to the wall behind it

70

indicated the prosperity of the town. Instead of sawdust on the floor, boards had been laid and painted. At the end of the room a small stage was raised and Thornton guessed that on a Saturday night it would provide space for a fiddler or two. Maybe one or two of the calico queens would put on a dance.

At this time of the day the saloon was empty save for four women wiping down tables and a short, fat man scrubbing down the bar. Over to Thornton's left behind a table sat a plump, fair-haired woman overseeing the work. In front of her sat a metal pot. She was sipping from a china mug.

Thornton crossed the saloon, his boots sounding on the boards, his spurs jingling. As he reached the table the woman looked up, a frown appearing on her heavily powdered face. 'You're mighty early, cowboy,' she said.

Thornton took a coin from his pocket and placed it on the table. 'That's for coffee; the rest is for you.'

She looked at the coin on the table, and pushed it back towards Thornton with her index finger. 'Give it to one of the girls. I gave up romancin' with cowboys a long time ago.'

Thornton turned, crossed to pick up a chair and a mug from the several which stood on the end of the bar. He came back to the woman, sat down and poured himself coffee from the pot. The woman looked at him intently, a slight frown on her face.

'I got some questions,' Thornton said. 'I'm guessin' you got answers.'

'I was wrong. You ain't no cowboy.'

'I'm lookin' for a man I got business with.'

'You gonna kill him?'

'Why'd you say that?'

'Ain't you the feller from the corral an' that shootin' yesterday?'

'Yes, an' Sheriff Landon's let me go, knowing I'm righteous.'

The woman nodded and took a sip of her coffee. 'Lottie's my name. Who you lookin' for?'

'Feller by the name o' Bart Morgan. Wears a big woolly jacket, an' a blue hat.'

'Hat like yourn? Same shape as a Stetson but with fancy trimming?'

'That's him.'

'I remember the hat. Don't see many of them that colour.'

Thornton took a sip of the coffee. After the hotel's coffee the black liquid before him tasted like buffalo dung. 'Morgan still around these parts?'

The woman gave him a calculated stare. 'Cost you another dollar.'

Thornton shrugged, dug in his pocket and placed a coin on the table. Her powdered hand swept it away into the folds of her skirt. She looked along the length of the saloon.

'Rosie!'

One of the young women turned away from the table she was wiping down and walked over to where Lottie and Thornton were seated.

'What is it, Lottie?'

Despite the dirty canvas apron the

73

girl wore to cover her skirts, and the tired look in her eyes, she was still young enough to be pretty, and it crossed Thornton's mind to wonder why she was working as a calico queen in the West. Rejected mail-order bride? Prey to the temptations of laudanum? She could be here for a dozen different reasons. They didn't concern him.

'I'm lookin' for Bart Morgan. Wears a big woollen jacket, blue Stetson.'

'I remember him. He was with me a week ago, day the train came in.'

'Is he still around?'

'Far as I know. He's taken over an old sheepman's shack, he tol' me.'

'You know where that is?'

Rosie shook her head. 'Can't help you there, mister.'

'I know where it is,' Lottie cut in. 'You get back to work now, Rosie.'

'Hold on.' Thornton again reached into his pocket. 'That's for you, Rosie.'

The girl looked down at the coin Thornton had handed her. 'Thanks, mister! Next time you're in, just ask for me. I'll show you a good time.'

'Sure,' Thornton said. For a moment he watched the girl walk back to the table and pick up a cloth. Then he turned back to Lottie.

'You're as likely to come in here for a woman as I am goin' to church,' Lottie said.

Thornton's mouth twitched. 'The old sheepman's shack?'

'Half a day's ride south. You'll see it to the west of a stand of cottonwoods. Nothin' else round those parts, so you'll not miss it.'

Thornton got to his feet. 'Thanks for the coffee.'

'What do we do if Morgan comes in here afore you meet up with him?'

'You an' Rosie keep your mouths shut or I'll be back.'

Lottie looked up suddenly, seeing the hard line of his mouth and the cold blue eyes. 'Sure, mister, sure,' she said quickly. 'We'll not say a word.'

\* \* \*

Butler appeared from out of one of the stalls as Thornton entered the livery. He was carrying a hay fork with wisps of hay on the tines, and nodded to himself as if seeing Thornton walking around free confirmed something he'd expected to see.

'Howdy, guess the sheriff let you go.' He half-turned to point along the barn. 'The roan's yourn if you've a mind to. I'll give you a good price for your mare. Your mount's over there.'

'We gotta deal, Mr Butler. The roan needs new plates, an' I've got some ridin' to do tomorrow, but I'll be comin' back to town. You easy with me ridin' the mare for a while?'

'Sure. I'll have new plates on the roan by first light tomorrow. I'll get the bills of sale written up and we'll settle up when you return the mare. Good to do business.'

'The schoolhouse close by?' Thornton asked him. He'd visit the bathhouse later.

'Past the corral at the end o' town.

Swing left and it's up on the rise.'

Thornton led the mare along the barn and through the high, wide-open doors. He stepped up to the saddle, and headed back to Main Street and the schoolhouse where he hoped to find an answer to how he'd spend the evening. It was too late to ride out to the sheepman's shack and he'd be best prepared to take on Morgan after a good night's sleep and a full belly.

Save for scuff marks on the soil in the corral where the body of Darvish had been dragged away there was no sign of the gunfight of the previous day. Thornton's quick glance was enough. He had no enthusiasm for dwelling on the man's death. If Darvish hadn't been so fast to reach for his gun he'd be alive today.

'Too late for that now,' Thornton said aloud, as he turned his mount's head to take the pathway running alongside the stand of cottonwoods. As he cleared the last line of trees he saw the schoolhouse standing on a slight incline.

Young boys in knee britches and stockings were piling out of the door of the school along with a group of little girls in cotton dresses. School was out for the day and the children flowed past him as he rode up to the building.

A few paces in front of the door, a young woman stood watching him approach. Thornton reined in, stepped down from his horse and touched the brim of his hat with a finger. The young woman was well dressed, a neat jacket above the skirt, which brushed at her leather shoes. A small cameo was pinned to her shirt at the throat. For a moment he wished he'd called at the bathhouse first.

'Howdy, ma'am. The name's Thornton. I came lookin' for the schoolmarm.'

The young woman smiled. 'Yes,' she said.

Thornton kept his face expressionless. Maybe the young woman didn't speak English too well. Since he'd arrived in town he'd heard lots of the townsfolk speaking in what he guessed

78

was Dutch or German. Maybe if he spoke more slowly she'd understand what he was saying.

'I guess I'm not explainin' too good, ma'am. I was hopin' to speak to the schoolmarm.'

She nodded. 'Yes, I'm the schoolmarm.'

For a second Thornton was silent. 'Oh, I thought you were too . . . ' He broke off to cover his awkwardness. 'I was hopin' to find a book to read. I've one to exchange,' he added quickly.

She smiled, showing even, white teeth. 'The general store stocks a pile of half-dime novels,' she said. 'I'm sure you'll find something there.'

'I guess I look like a saddle-tramp, ma'am. But I hope I ain't thinkin' like one.' He turned to thrust his hand into his saddle-bag and pulled out the book he'd finished in jail that morning.

'I'd be happy for you to have this for one of yourn.'

She took the book from his hand, opened the leather cover and glanced at the title. Then she looked up, her eyes sparkling. 'Forgive me, Mr Thornton. You're in luck. I've a couple of Mr Cooper's novels, and I haven't read this one. I'll willingly exchange.'

She did have a beautiful smile, he thought. But why the heck was she doin' a schoolmarm's job in a western town? He glanced down at her hand but her fingers were ringless. Some buckaroo around Alveston would win himself a real fine bride.

'Mebbe you could leave the book at the Majestic. I'm stayin' there afore ridin' out tomorrow.'

'Then you'll have to come to the Box Social tonight!'

Thornton frowned slightly. 'Ma'am, I don't even know what a Box Social is.'

'They're great fun, Mr Thornton, and money is raised to help the poor people of the town for when winter returns. There's dancing, and all the ladies make up a supper box and the men bid for a box, not knowing the owner. Then the lady shares her supper with the winning bidder.'

'An' all the town attends?'

'Yes,' she said. A faint blush showed on her cheeks.

'I'll be there,' Thornton said. 'Bring the book this evening. It'll save you a trip to the Majestic.' He touched the brim of his hat. 'You mind tellin' me your name?'

Her cheeks turned a deeper pink. 'Hetty Jordan.' She paused. 'Miss Hetty Jordan.'

Thornton rode back to the livery, a smile on his face. He'd spend a couple of hours at the town's shindig. What was it called? A Box Social, that was it. He probably wouldn't get to sharing Hetty Jordan's supper box but he might be able to accompany her in a dance.

Butler took his horse and Thornton unhitched his saddle-bag, picked up his Winchester and walked back along Main Street to the general store, where he bought new pants and a couple of shirts. No point in turning up at a Box Social in Levis and a woollen shirt.

His business with the storekeeper finished, he carried on along the boardwalk to Landon's office. The sheriff was behind his desk, a puzzled frown on his face, examining the sidearm on his desk. He looked up as Thornton stepped further into the office.

'You tol' me you were leavin' town.'

'Morgan's still around.'

'Then make sure you're outta town when you shoot him.' He gestured at the sidearm on his desk. 'I was tryin' to figure what Darvish was totin'. Mighty fancy-lookin'.'

Thornton pulled the gun towards him. 'It's a Smith & Wesson Russian. The marshal down in Abilene carries one.'

Landon raised his eyebrows. 'You bin around some.'

Thornton shrugged. 'Yeah, I guess so. Even get to goin' to a Box Social tonight.'

'You know how a Box Social works?'

'Yeah. Miss Hetty Jordan tol' me about it.'

Landon raised his eyebrows. 'Did she, by heck?' He grinned. 'Get your money ready. A coupla glasses of the mayor's punch an' folks get real feisty. I run the party an' some o' the townsfolk'll bid up to ten dollars for a supper. Mighty good cause, though.'

'Mebbe I can start the pot.' Thornton thrust his hand into the pocket of his shirt, and brought out a couple of coins. 'Always like a good cause.'

Five minutes later when he left the sheriff's office he had a broad smile on his weather-beaten face.

# 5

Thornton was fifty yards from the big barn at the end of town when he heard the music. The barn doors must have been pinned back for the sound swept along Main Street, prompting some of the townsfolk heading in the same direction to burst into song. Despite the reasons bringing Thornton to the town he couldn't help warming to the happy atmosphere.

As he got closer to the barn he realized the townsfolk must have put down boards for the dancers as the sounds of boots hitting wood resonated along the street. He reached the wide opening to the barn and handed over his fifty cents to join the party.

Three sets were on the floor for a quadrille and the barn shook with the efforts of the dancers. The floor was rough, the music a trifle jerky, but every dancer whirled around with abandon. A small platform had been erected at the end of the barn, on which sat the four musicians — three fiddlers and a squeezebox player. In front of them stood Sheriff Landon calling the dance.

'*Alemane left. Right hand to pardner, an' grand right and left. Everybody swing.*'

Thornton looked around. Hetty Jordan hadn't exactly said she'd be there but he would have been dumb not to cotton on. He couldn't see her among the men and women who stood around the dancers, waiting to rush on the floor and take the places of those who were about to finish.

At the end of the barn a table had been set up on which stood two huge bowls, and Thornton guessed they were holding the punch Landon had mentioned to him. At the last shindig like this he'd attended over in Powder River two similar bowls of punch had been provided. One contained fruit juice and home-made lemonade. The other must have included black powder although

Moreton Frewen assured him it was only whiskey from Scotland. Whatever, Thornton felt like he'd been kicked by a mule the day after. He went to the table and pointed at the bowls.

'They both safe?'

The fair-headed man behind the table grinned. 'If you're temperant, sir, take the one on the left. You may choose to call a halt after a coupla glasses from the other.'

'Thanks for the tip.' He was pouring himself a glass when he heard his name spoken behind him.

'Mr Thornton, sir?'

Thornton turned to see a fresh-faced young man smiling at him. Men and women milled around him as the music came to a halt, Landon and the others taking a rest.

'The name is Henry Wilson, sir. The Reverend Jordan asks if you would join his table.'

'I'll do that, Henry, and don't call me sir. Makes me feel old. The name's Brad.'

'I'll show you the way, sir, erm, Brad.'

Thornton followed the young man down the length of the barn, threading his way through the townsfolk and heading past where Landon and the musicians stood on a raised platform. As Thornton drew level with the platform he glanced across. Landon gave a brief nod of recognition.

The two men reached the large table set against the wall of the barn. A dozen men and women looked Thornton's way. In the middle of the line of seats, his back against the wall, sat a grey-haired man wearing a western jacket over a silk vest and shirt. A silk bow flopped on to his chest. Thornton couldn't help thinking that the Reverend Jordan, for surely it was he, might have looked more comfortable in his church-going clothes.

'Mr Brad Thornton,' Wilson announced.

'Kind of you to invite me, Reverend,' Thornton said.

'Take a seat, Mr Thornton. You can greet everyone here later. I hear you've already met my daughter, Hetty.'

'We have a mutual admiration for Mr James Fenimore Cooper,' Thornton said.

Jordan smiled. 'Ah, yes! *The Deerslayer*. A fine book. Are you in Alveston on business, sir?'

'I have to meet with a man.'

'Then we shall see you in church on Sunday, I hope.'

Hetty touched her father's arm. 'Now, Papa. You're here to enjoy yourself, not to build your congregation.'

'You're right, my dear. I just — ' He broke off and looked over Thornton's shoulder. 'Young Walker! Good to see you, Luke. I trust your father is in good heart.'

Thornton turned to see a young man in his early twenties dressed in range clothes, which had probably been bought in one of the better shops in Cheyenne.

'My father is most well, Reverend.'

'I hear you're to spend a year in Cheyenne.'

'Yes, my father wishes me to learn more about the ranching business.' He looked down at Thornton. 'My father would like to have a few moments to talk with Mr Thornton.'

'Sure,' Thornton said. 'I'm here.'

He felt Hetty squeeze his arm beneath the cloth that covered the table. Not the right answer, he realized. He got to his feet, wondering what Walker could wish to discuss.

'J.T. Walker's the richest rancher in the county. The Bar J is huge. Some say he's the richest man in the Territory,' Hetty whispered.

Thornton grinned. 'Then I'd better find out what he wants.'

He followed Luke Walker across the barn. They reached a long table that dominated one end of the barn and which had clearly been specially placed for the Walker party. Around the table were seated an even number of men and women. There was no mistaking J.T. Walker although Thornton had never laid eyes on the man before. Walker's broadcloth jacket covered wide shoulders and a deep chest. For his age, maybe some sixty years, he still looked a powerful man. His shock of iron-grey hair topped bushy eyebrows in a weather-beaten face. Between thick lips jutted a long, thin cheroot; unlit, Thornton supposed, in deference to the ladies seated around him.

Walker waved a large hand. 'Take a seat, Thornton. I've a proposition for you.'

Thornton took his seat and looked across the table at Walker. A man who was used to getting what he wanted, he decided. No courtesies. It was straight to business.

'I've been talking with Sheriff Landon about you, Thornton. Landon is a good judge of men, an' he thinks highly of you.'

Thornton's mouth twitched. 'So highly he threw me in jail.'

'Yeah, I heard about that. All a misunderstandin', so I've been told.' Walker took the cheroot from his mouth. 'How d'you fancy comin' to work for me?'

'Ranchin' is not what I'm about.'

'I ain't talkin' about ranchin'. It's your gun I'm buyin'.'

The eldest of the women at the table stood up abruptly, the other women following suit. She placed a hand on Walker's shoulder as the men clambered to their feet. 'I think, John, I'll take the ladies away for a few moments.'

Walker patted her hand, not put out for a second. 'Of course, my dear.'

The women were barely five yards away and the men back in their seats when Walker turned back to Thornton.

'I ain't tryin' to turn my back on progress, but the railroad's gonna be bringin' in dirt-farmers an' they're gonna be looking at the open range. I need all the land I got for my beef an' I'll need a good man to take care of my interests.' He stared hard at Thornton. 'I pay good money, so what do you say?'

'I have a job, working for an Englishman over at Powder Creek.'

'You talkin about Moreton Frewen? Well now, there's happenstance. Feller's married to my eldest daughter, Maude. Frewen's a good man but he ain't a real cattleman. All these Englishmen wanna do is go out huntin'. Come an' work for a real rancher.'

'Mr Frewen knows ranching. He's bringing Hereford cattle from England an' crossing them with longhorns. Reckons he's gonna make a lot of money.'

'Is he, by hell?' Walker stared hard at Thornton. 'Mebbe I'll take a look at that notion. What was the name of that English cattle you spoke of?'

'Hereford. I believe it's named after territory in England.' Thornton got to his feet. 'I appreciate your offer but I'll wait until I've finished working for Mr Frewen. We can talk again. Good evening, Mr Walker.'

He crossed the barn again and took his seat alongside Hetty as the group of musicians played a little fanfare. He leaned across to Hetty. 'Walker offered me a job,' he said.

She opened her mouth to reply but before she could do so the voice of Sheriff Landon rang down the length of the barn. 'Gentlemen! Now we got to the time when you give to the good people in Alveston who ain't been fortunate so far in their endeavours.' He picked up a supper box tied with pink ribbon. 'Who's gonna be the first lucky feller? What am I bid?'

'Fifty cents,' came a shout, to be greeted with mock howls of derision.

'A dollar,' called out Luke Walker.

'Two dollars!'

Landon swung around, facing each side of the barn in turn. 'Gentlemen, check your pocketbooks. This box has been prepared by the prettiest girl in town.' He paused dramatically. 'I ain't sayin' who's the prettiest gal in Alveston. I ain't that brave!'

And so it went on, to the amusement of everyone in the barn. Landon certainly knew how to get money out of the townsmen, Thornton decided. He was about to take a sip of his punch when he saw Landon nod briefly in his direction.

'OK, folks! A few boxes left,' he called. 'Here's one to get out your money.'

Thornton listened to the few opening bids. But then there was a gasp from the crowd as a strong voice called out, 'Ten dollars!'

'That's Carl Fredericks,' somebody shouted.

'He owns the Lazy Y ranch,' Hetty said.

'Can't see that bein' beaten, Carl,' called Landon. 'I — '

'Fifteen!' Thornton called.

A shout of amazement ran through the crowd. Who was bidding a chunk of his money for supper with someone he might never speak with again?

'Twenty,' Fredericks called, and an excited buzz of chatter ran around the crowd.

'You gonna tell 'em the rules, Sheriff?' a townsman called out.

'Sure am,' Landon said. 'Don't fergit folks, a feller has to come up with the bid here an' now. The cash or a note.'

'Tell 'em what happens if they can't meet their bid.' A woman's voice this time and Thornton guessed all the townsfolk knew the answer as a great cheer erupted.

'The men get together an' throw him in the dung heap, end o' town.' Landon's explanation was again met with a huge cheer. 'It's down to Carl at twenty dollars.'

'Thirty dollars,' Thornton called out.

A further murmur of excitement ran around the men and women. The town hadn't held such an exciting Box Social since the blacksmith got drunk and punched a drummer from Cheyenne who'd got too fancy with his wife.

Landon looked across at Fredericks. 'Down to you, Carl.'

His mouth set in a tight line, Fredericks shook his head.

'Then Mr Thornton has his supper with . . . ' Landon paused, looking at a sheet of paper. Then he looked up to announce the owner of the supper box. 'Folks, Mr Thornton's gonna have supper with the young lady who stepped in to save the school when the schoolmarm skedaddled with her cowboy. Ladies and gentlemen, Miss Hetty Jordan!'

A burst of applause filled the barn as a young boy, carrying the supper box, came across to the Jordan table. 'There's a table ready for you and Miss Jordan, sir. I got it ready myself,' he said proudly.

Thornton slipped a coin into the boy's hand. 'Don't spend it all on candy.'

The boy looked down. 'Jeepers! Thank you, sir! I'll not do that!'

'Reverend Jordan, ladies and gentlemen.'

The speaker was behind him and Thornton turned to see Carl Fredericks standing a few feet away greeting the group at the table. Fredericks didn't look at him. Instead, he looked at Hetty, who was standing alongside Thornton, her hand on his arm.

'I guess you didn't think you'd be havin' supper with a gunslinger, Miss Hetty,' Fredericks said.

Thornton felt Hetty's hand tighten on his arm, but he had no intention of answering Fredericks's challenge. From the look in the rancher's eyes Thornton suspected that the younger man had taken more than a couple of glasses of the punch.

'I guess we both got reason to be mad, Mr Fredericks,' he said cheerfully. 'Sheriff roped us both in, I reckon.' He shrugged. 'It's good to know that some brats are gonna be wearin' shoes this winter.'

'I reckon you'll be better off back in Powder River,' Fredericks snapped. He turned on his heel and strode away in the direction of his table.

Hetty looked up at Thornton, a quizzical smile on her face.

'Did you both bribe the sheriff?'

Thornton grinned. 'That's agin the law.' He touched her hand for a moment. 'Now let me see what you've given us for supper.'

* * *

Thornton walked away from the church house, a book tugging at the pocket of his trail jacket, humming a tune beneath his breath. His sister had told him when they were young together in Boston that he couldn't carry a tune in a bucket, and he had to admit when he was older that she was right. But there was something to the music at the Box Social that had stuck in his head.

His musical efforts stopped abruptly when he remembered that the following day he was likely to be up against Bart Morgan. There was talk of Morgan killing a lawman in the west of the Territory and then escaping from jail. If he was holed up in the sheepman's shack he was there for a reason. The town's bank could be his target but surely Landon and the Volunteers would be too much of a challenge.

Thornton resumed his humming as he turned off Main Street into the shadows of the alleyway which would take him to the Majestic and the room he'd booked earlier in the day. A good soft bed would be welcome after a night on the bunk in the jail, and before that, nights on hard ground with his head on a saddle and a only a thin blanket covering him.

'Hold it there, Thornton!'

Out of the shadows stepped three men, broad shapes outlined in the moonlight penetrating the alleyway. Thornton backed off a couple of paces. He didn't need good light to recognize a threat.

'What can I do for you?'

A snicker came from the biggest of the three. 'You can learn some manners. Makin' a fool of our boss ain't somethin' we care for in Alveston.'

Thornton blew breath from between pursed lips. For pity's sake! Three liquored-up cowboys from Fredericks's ranch. He reached down to his boot and pulled out his pocket pistol. Taking care not to hit any of the three he fired into the dirt of the alley. There was a crack of noise and a thud as the slug bit into the ground.

'This here in my hand,' Thornton said in a tone that he could have been using with Warren Jenkins, the stage-owner, 'is a hammerless .32. I shoot one of you, and the slug will rattle 'round in your skull until it comes out of an eye. Who's gonna be first?'

'The boss was right! You are a goddamned gunhawk!'

'You got five seconds to get out o' my way. One, two . . .'

Ten minutes later Thornton was beneath cotton sheets at the Majestic, smoking a last roll-up for the day and planning how best to take on Bart Morgan.

# 6

Thornton was out of the hotel and on to Main Street soon after dawn where he found the day's business of the town already underway. Doors to the stores were being flung open, shutters turned back. Sparks were flying from the blacksmith's anvil and cowboys, having spent a night in the Silver Horse, were riding out to the range. Butler from the livery was walking a chestnut mare down Main Street and he raised a hand in greeting as Thornton crossed the street.

The Chinaman's place was filling up but Thornton was able to grab a table where he had a clear view of the door. He didn't expect Morgan to come bursting in, pistol in hand, but there was no point in taking chances. One or two of the townsfolk at the other tables looked across at him, curious to know what this stranger was about in their town. Thornton looked around for his food, avoiding their stares.

The Chinaman's boy brought him fried salt pork and beans, with sourdough biscuits, and a mug of strong black coffee. He could be in for a day's hard riding and it was wise to start on a full stomach, not knowing when he'd have the chance to eat again. While he cut into the generous portion of meat he again turned over in his mind why Morgan had holed up close to Alveston.

The only answer could be that Morgan was planning a big job. Yet Alveston was unlikely to offer any target that wouldn't be strongly defended. Could he be thinking of attacking the stage? But if Jenkins was shipping valuable cargo he'd have made plans to protect it.

He took a gulp of the hot coffee. Maybe he'd be wise to watch the sheepman's shack for a few days. Maybe Morgan's movements would give him a clue as to what the no-good was planning. A shadow fell across his table and he looked up. To his surprise, Warren Jenkins was standing over him.

'You mind if I join you, Mr Thornton?' Jenkins said.

'Take a seat.'

Thornton looked across the room and held up his coffee in the direction of the boy serving the tables. Promptly, the boy brought across the coffee pot and a further mug for Jenkins as the stage-owner sat down.

'I guess you'll be off to South Pass this morning,' Thornton said.

Jenkins breathed in deeply. 'And that's why I'm here. I need to ask a favour of you.'

'Ask away, Mr Jenkins.'

'The U.P. arrives in town in a couple of hours. I've a stage going north that will pick up a couple of passengers from the train. They're the ladies of powerful men in Cheyenne. It's important they reach their destination in a timely fashion.'

'So what's the problem?'

'Fletcher, who rides shotgun, is sick, and there's no one else to take his place.'

'And you want me to help out?'

'Only to the first station and then you can return to town on the stage heading this way. You'd be back here before nightfall.' Jenkins grimaced with frustration. 'I know this is not the sort of task you'd normally take on, but the reputation of my stage line depends on those two ladies.'

'You carryin' anythin' valuable on the stages? Gold, maybe?'

Jenkins raised his eyebrows. 'Nothing like that. I have shipped gold to the bank before but then I hire half a dozen of the Volunteers to ride as guards. Both north and south stages will carry only passengers.'

Thornton did a swift mental calculation. From all he'd learned, Morgan was not a man to go after the purses of townsfolk. He'd been after Morgan for several weeks; another day was of little concern. He'd made a promise to

Jenkins and he intended to keep it.

'I'll ride shotgun for you,' he said. 'I've business out of town but that can wait. After all,' he added, 'if you hadn't put in a word for me I'd still be in jail.'

Jenkins let go a deep sigh of obvious relief. 'Thank you, Mr Thornton. Joey French will be driving the stage. He's a good man and I can rely on him. He'll fix it to be outside the office half an hour before he's ready to roll. There'll be a scattergun for you but we're not expecting any trouble.'

Thornton looked at the morning light being thrown by the early sun through the open door. 'Looks a fine day for a ride. I'll make sure I greet the passengers and help them when needed.'

Jenkins smiled. 'The ladies should be quite taken with their new shotgun.'

* * *

Exactly half an hour before the U.P. was due, Thornton saw the Concord slow to a halt in Main Street. Built in the town of the same name in his home state of Massachusetts he'd seen Concords often enough when he'd been at West Point. He walked along the boardwalk to greet the short, weather-beaten man climbing down from the stage.

'Joey French, I guess,' said Thornton, stretching out a hand.

'An' you must be Brad Thornton,' French said, vigorously shaking Thornton's hand. 'Mr Jenkins tol' me you were gonna be ridin' shotgun.'

'Just to the first station.'

'Yeah, the shotgun comin' south will change with you, an' you can ride as shotgun back here. You OK with that?'

'That's fine. You want a hand with anything?'

'Nope, got it all sorted. You gonna ride with me, you gotta answer a coupla questions.'

'Ask away.'

'Can you read an' write? Shotgun from this town can barely write his name. Any paper an' I gotta do it.'

'I can handle that,' Thornton said,

trying not to smile.

'You know how to drive six horses?'

'I reckon I'm smarter with my letters but I could stop 'em.'

'That's all it takes. I allus check with a new feller.'

Thornton grinned. 'Let's hope I don't need to.' He turned to examine the stagecoach. 'Fancy rig you got here.'

In the morning sun the red body of the Concord gleamed against its yellow underside. The wheels appeared to be made of white oak. On the door facing Thornton an artist had painted, with fine brushstrokes, a green landscape. Leather curtains showed at the coach's sides.

'Cost Mr Jenkins eleven hundred dollars,' French said proudly.

In the distance came the hoot of the U.P. engine, and French turned away from the coach. 'I'll pick up the mail. There's a coupla gen'men in the office who are travellin'. A boy will bring around the bags of the two ladies from Cheyenne, an' there'll be a maid with 'em. We'll get 'em on board and we'll leave on the hour.' He looked over Thornton's shoulder. 'Sheriff's here, likes to show his face when we got important travellers.'

Thornton turned. 'Good day, Sheriff.'

'You leavin' us, Thornton? Can't say I'm sorry.'

Thornton grinned. 'You got it wrong. I'm ridin' shotgun for Warren Jenkins just to the first station. Comin' back to town on the other stage. Then I'll be leaving tomorrow.'

'We ain't had a hold-up for more than five years. Don't you get shootin' for the fun of it.'

'I'm just gonna enjoy the ride, Mr Landon.'

There was the noise of wheels on the boardwalk and from around the corner of the building appeared a boy pushing a handcart on top of which were piled four bags. Behind the cart walked three women, two of them in rich silks which showed through their open travelling coats. A more modestly dressed younger woman walked a few paces behind them.

'Welcome to Alveston, ladies,' Landon said, as the two women reached the coach. 'We'd have liked to offer you hospitality but I understand you're anxious to be on your way.'

Thornton stepped forward and introduced himself. 'If there's anything you need, ladies, the hotel is ready to accommodate you. We shall be leaving in thirty minutes. All your bags will be safe with us.'

The older of the two women stepped forward to address Thornton. 'Are you working for Mr Jenkins?'

'No, ma'am. I'm just riding shotgun to the first station.'

'Mr Thornton is an ex-US Marshal,' Landon said, poker-faced. 'He's checking out security for Mr Jenkins.'

'We had a moment with Mr Jenkins before the train left. He didn't mention your name, Mr Thornton.'

Thornton shrugged. 'Part of his service, ladies. I don't s'pose Mr Jenkins even thought it worth mentioning.'

'C'mon, boy. Let's get those bags put away,' French said.

Landon and Thornton stood together as the two ladies walked the few yards to the hotel. 'I ain't sure if it's you or Warren Jenkins who owes me whiskey,' Landon said.

★ ★ ★

As the old railroad clock pinned to the wall of the stagecoach office reached ten o'clock the stage jolted into movement and the six horses driven by Joey French set off down Main Street at a walk. French, supported by a straw-filled sack beneath him, sat on an equal level to Thornton, who held the scattergun close by his side.

A few of the townsfolk stopped on the boardwalk to wave as the stage passed them and Thornton wondered what life was like driving one of these superb coaches across thousands of miles. Soon, he supposed, Joey French and his like would pass into history as the railroad stretched its iron tentacles wider and wider across the country.

'You been drivin' stages for a while, Joey?'

The little man snickered. 'For longer than I like to remember. But I got no family an' don't s'pose I ever will. This suits me fine. I had ten years' drivin' Concords over the Sierra Nevadas but you gotta be young doin' that.'

'You ever come across Charlie Parkhurst?' Thornton asked. 'I've heard of him drivin' six-in-hands over the Nevadas.'

'Sure, most folks in California, mebbe the whole of the country's heard of Charlie.' Joey pulled back his lips in a grin. 'Only, what most folks don't know is Charlie ain't a 'him'; Charlie's a 'her'.'

'A woman?'

'Damn right. Made me swear to keep my mouth shut. So don't you go talkin' 'bout such matters.'

Thornton stifled a smile, tempted to ask how Joey had discovered her secret but thinking it better not to pursue the subject. 'You got any advice for me while I'm ridin' with you?'

'If you're gonna chew baccy, make sure you're spittin' with the wind,' Joey said. 'That's all I reckon I can tell you. You don't look as if you need tellin' about the scattergun or that big Colt on your hip.'

'You can tell me somethin' about the horses,' Thornton said.

'Not a lot to tell.' He raised his hand holding the rein a few inches. 'You can see how this jerk-line runs through to the lead hosses. A single steady pull and the lead hoss'll go left. I give the line a coupla jerks an' the lead hoss'll go right. Behind the leaders we got the swingers and then the wheelers. The pairs do different jobs, that's all.'

But for not a lot to tell, Joey was content to impart as much knowledge as he could of driving stages across the land. After three hours, Thornton reckoned he knew more about stage travel than Wells Fargo and although Joey had made it interesting he wasn't

112

sorry when Joey paused in mid-tale and pointed behind Thornton.

'Hand me that old brass bugle, an' we'll let Bill Hobbes know we're on our way.'

Thornton groped behind the seat until his hand fell on the shiny metal. He handed the bugle across to Joey, who put it to his mouth and, for a small man, blew a blast that assaulted Thornton's ears. There was a short pause, and from a distant bugle came an answering call.

'Bill's aready for us,' Joey said, handing back the bugle.

He flicked the jerk-line and barked an order at the lead horses. They quickened their pace as they headed around a bend in the trail, enabling Thornton to see the cluster of buildings and corrals which marked, for him, the end of his journey north.

'Bill's wife'll have grub ready for us. The other stage should be here in less than an hour,' French said. 'It's been good to have you as shotgun, Mr

Thornton.' His toothless mouth opened in a grin. 'I guess you don't do this often.'

'I've enjoyed it too, Joey. And I know a lot more about coaches — ' He broke off as he saw Joey's frown. 'What's wrong?'

Joey was staring in the direction of the stage station now only a few hundred yards away. 'Bill's allus out front when we arrive. Big feller, sports a long grey beard.' He brought the horses down to a walk as the coach passed the edge of a corral, which held maybe two dozen change horses. 'Mebbe somethin's wrong in the house.'

Thornton picked up the scattergun from down beside his leg as Joey brought the coach to a halt. 'Stay here, Joey. I'll take a look.' He jumped lightly to the ground, and stood for a moment beside the coach. 'Nothing to worry about, folks. Mr Hobbes must be busy in the house.'

He advanced on the house, the door of which was closed, holding the scattergun across his chest. A threat from any direction could be met by a rapid swing of the weapon. He halted thirty feet from the house.

'Bill Hobbes! Can you hear me?'

There was a pause. 'I hear you. I got trouble in here. But you're OK. C'mon in.'

Still cautious, Thornton approached the house. Using the barrel end of the scattergun he pushed open the door. Against the opposite wall of the room on to which the door opened stood a tall, elderly man sporting a grey beard that fell to his black vest. Thornton stepped in.

'Joey was gettin' — ' He broke off as he felt the barrel of a sidearm press heavily against his neck.

A rasping voice from behind him gave an order. 'Blackie, take this cowboy's scattergun. An' you,' the gun pressing hard against Thornton's neck, 'walk a coupla paces an' drop that gunbelt. You make a move an' it'll be your last.'

'There's five soldiers on the stage,'

Thornton said. 'You're gonna die here.'

'No I ain't,' scoffed the voice. 'There's two old-timers and two ladies with their maid from Cheyenne. Now move, an' get that gunbelt off!'

Thornton did as ordered. He moved into the centre of the cabin, a few paces from Hobbes. Unbuckling his gunbelt he lowered it to the floor.

'OK, now turn around.'

Thornton turned, took one look at the man who held his pistol aimed at him and thought it was his last moment on earth. In front of him, a pace ahead of two other men, stood a tall, broad-shouldered man wearing a thick woollen coat and an unusual blue Dakota hat. Thornton swallowed a couple of times, trying to keep his face expressionless. His life wasn't worth five cents if Bart Morgan realized that in front of him he had the man who had shot one of his brothers, jailed the other and killed Jack Darvish.

'Blackie! Empty this cowboy's weapons an' give 'em back to him,' Morgan ordered one of the men. 'Cowboy, you're gonna go back out there an' tell all those folks everything's fine.'

'An' if I don't?'

Morgan looked hard at him for a second. 'We'll kill you an' all the folks on the stage.'

'You're gonna kill us all anyways.'

Morgan shook his head. 'You think I'm stupid? I ain't aimin' to kill anyone,' he barked. 'But you're beginnin' to make me think agin.'

Thornton was silent for a second, and then he nodded. 'OK, I'll bring them in.'

Morgan leered. 'Once you've tol' 'em, you come back here. Blackie, give him his scattergun an' his Colt.' He pointed at Hobbes, who hadn't moved from near the wall. 'You get close to the door, so they can see you, an' remember we got your woman in the back room. You don't wanna have me visitin' her.'

A couple of minutes later Thornton stepped out of the gloom of the house into the midday light. He saw Joey

French standing up at the front of the coach looking anxiously towards the house. He'd made no move to unhitching and changing the horses.

'It's OK, Joey,' Thornton called, holding aloft his scattergun. 'Hobbes had a problem with Mrs Hobbes.'

Joey jumped down to the ground and opened the door of the coach as Thornton turned on his heel and walked back into the house.

'Get away from the door,' Morgan ordered. 'Let 'em get right in here. Hobbes, you open the door for 'em, an' then stand back.'

Grim-faced, the station-keeper moved to open the door as the five passengers and French walked the few yards from the stagecoach to the house.

'Say your piece, Hobbes,' Morgan ordered from behind the door.

'Food's on the table, folks. Sorry for takin' the time.'

Joey French led the passengers into the house. He frowned as he saw the long table in the centre of the room bare of food. 'What's goin' on, Bill . . . ?'

He broke off as Morgan stepped from the shadows behind the open door, his sidearm held at arm's length, shifting his aim backwards and forwards across the group, who huddled together, white faces registering their shock.

'All of you sit 'round the table,' Morgan barked. 'We're gonna do everythin' normal. You don't try anythin' stupid, an' you'll be OK.'

Exchanging frightened glances, the passengers slowly moved across the room to take their places at the table. Morgan turned to Joey French.

'You sit one end o' the table,' he ordered. 'Shotgun, you get over in that corner. Blackie, hold a gun on him,' he barked at the man whose face was marked with a pink stain. 'He makes a move, you shoot him.'

Thornton did as he was told, moving into the shadowy corner of the room, closely followed by Blackie, who held his pistol to his back. Thornton was puzzled. What the hell was Morgan up to? If he was intending to rob the stage he was going at it in a roundabout way.

Morgan turned to Hobbes. 'Get your woman and have her put food on the table. Any tricks an' it'll be these folks who'll pay.'

'You'll hang for this, you blackguard!'

Morgan turned to the elderly woman who had spoken out, her face defiant even as he moved closer to where she sat. 'One more word outta you an' it'll be your last,' he snarled. His hard eyes rested on the woman, seeming to notice for the first time her gold chain. His hand strayed towards her throat. 'Now, ain't that pretty.'

'You lay a finger on the lady an' you'll have a dozen Pinkerton agents after you,' Thornton called. 'These two ladies are the wives of senior judges in Cheyenne.'

Morgan spun on his heel, bringing up his sidearm to aim at Thornton, blood rushing to his face. For a few seconds an icy silence descended around the table. Thornton swallowed as he saw Morgan's knuckles tighten. Then the taller of the two men with Morgan spoke.

'Mebbe we should think about what we're here for, Bart. You wantin' everything normal, an' all.'

'I'll get the grub,' said Hobbes hurriedly.

Morgan slowly lowered his sidearm. Not taking his eyes off Thornton he edged closer to the taller of the two who had spoken.

'What did you say to me?' Morgan snarled, his eyes still on Thornton.

'I just said we should think about why we're here.' For a big man his voice was weak, and his words came out almost in a whisper.

'When I wanna hear from you, I'll tell you!'

Morgan's free hand came up fast and he back-handed the man across his face, sending him staggering against the wall of the cabin. Cries of protest came from around the table, quickly cut off as Morgan spun around to face them.

'Shut your goddamn mouths!'

'I should be changin' the hosses, you want everythin' normal,' said Joey quickly. 'That feller could give me a hand.'

Morgan breathed in deeply, as if deliberately making an effort to calm himself. 'OK, go do it,' he barked. 'Then we wait for the stage comin' south.'

'You're makin' a mistake, mister,' Joey said. 'There ain't nothin' worth stealin' on that stage. Coupla passengers is all they got, an' they ain't gonna be carryin' much.'

To Thornton's surprise, Morgan leered at French with a smile which didn't show any humour. 'You're wrong, little man. There's gold on that stage, an' I'm gonna take it!'

# 7

Not one word had been spoken around the table since Hobbes's wife, ashen-faced, had brought in food and placed it before the travellers. Thornton was turning over in his mind Morgan's reasoning for such a move. Were there travellers, maybe armed guards, with the stage coming south? Was Morgan planning to have them enter the station house without suspecting anything was amiss? But if that was the case, Morgan would be taking them on alone, as the two men with him looked unlikely to be useful in a gunfight. Reluctantly, he decided he could only wait and see what developed.

Thornton had exchanged glances with Joey when the driver had returned from changing the horses but Joey had given him a quick shake of the head: there was nothing he could do. Any rash attempt to disarm Morgan could lead to a bloodbath and innocent passengers being killed.

Was the stage-owner playing a double game? Maybe there really was gold on the stage and Jenkins had reckoned he needed stronger protection for the last stretch of the coach's journey into town. Aware that Thornton was in his debt, had he taken advantage of the situation and recruited him to add, unknowingly, further protection for a gold shipment?

The sound of a distant bugle prompted worried glances between the passengers around the table. Thornton knew he would soon have answers to his questions. Morgan stood up from the stool on which he'd sat for over an hour without saying a word.

'Everyone sit tight, an' no noise,' he barked. 'Hobbes, get out there an' give 'em your bugle sound. An' this time stay out there an' lead 'em in. You warn 'em off, an' your woman dies first.'

Hobbes nodded, without saying a

word, and took down the bugle from the shelf above his head. He looked around at the table, his eyes apparently searching for those of his wife, who had been forced to sit at the table after she'd served the food, which remained on the table untouched. Hobbes managed a strained smile of encouragement before turning away and heading out of the cabin. Through the open door, Thornton saw him raise the bugle to his lips and sound the answering call.

'Blackie! Jed! Get in the corner outta sight,' Morgan barked. 'I'll get behind the door like last time. Leave the shotgun to me, he starts anythin'.'

The two men moved to the corner of the room as the noise of the approaching stagecoach grew louder and Thornton could hear the hoofs of the horses thudding on the dirt of the trail. Hobbes remained where he was outside, a few yards from the door of the cabin, the bugle held at arm's length by his side. The shouts of the driver's orders to the horses could now be clearly heard as the stagecoach approached the first corral, the horses slowing to a walk.

'Howdy, Bill! Your missus got the grub on the table?' the driver called out.

'Everythin's ready for you, Cisco,' Hobbes called back.

The driver and his shotgun jumped to the ground. Through the door of the cabin Thornton could see that neither was armed, the shotgun having left his scattergun on the stage.

'An hour's break for food, sir,' Thornton heard the shotgun say, as he opened the door of the coach. 'You'll find everything you'll need here.'

Thornton saw a smartly dressed man in city clothes about his own age step down from the coach, followed by a young boy in britches and stockings and a woollen jacket. They both stretched their limbs after the confines of the coach and moved to follow the driver and shotgun towards Hobbes and the cabin.

'Food on the table,' said Hobbes.

'Ready for you.'

'You all keep your mouths shut,' warned Morgan in a low voice.

As the four, followed by Hobbes, reached the cabin, both the shotgun and the driver stood aside to allow the boy and the man to enter first. 'Good day, ladies and gentlemen,' the man greeted the group around the table. He and the boy moved further into the cabin, allowing the driver and the shotgun to enter.

'Hold it right there!' Morgan shouted. 'You make a move an' it'll be your last!'

Shocked, all four newcomers stood still, staring at Morgan, whose sidearm was aimed at them. 'You back off to the end of the cabin,' Morgan ordered. 'I ain't aimin' to kill anyone here but you do somethin' stupid an' you're gonna die.'

Thornton caught the look in the eyes of the newcomer with the boy and saw that he was contemplating an attack on Morgan. Then, as if the man had decided the cost would be too great, his expression altered. Instead, he put a defensive hand on the boy's shoulder.

The boy turned, and Thornton felt as if he'd been kicked in the stomach by a mule.

The once-pale features, now marked by the sun, and the high forehead were unmistakeable. The last time Thornton had seen him was at Powder River when they'd ridden together to witness the branding. If William Frewen identified him Morgan would know that he, Thornton, was more than just a shotgun.

'You're makin' a mistake, mister,' the newly arrived driver said. 'We ain't carryin' stuff you'd wanna steal.'

Morgan ignored him. Instead, he looked around the cabin, apparently satisfying himself that everything was under control. Blackie stood by the wall opposite the door leading outside, his weapon held loosely in his hand. Thornton was aware that the other no-good was behind him.

Morgan gestured with his sidearm. 'C'mon and stand by me, boy!'

Eyes wide with fear, the boy turned to face Morgan. Thornton breathed a silent prayer of thanks for the shadows around him that prevented the boy from seeing him clearly. The boy's companion tightened his hold on William's shoulder.

'You harm the boy and you'll swing from a scaffold by the end of the year.'

'You talk kinda quaint, mister,' Morgan sneered. 'Reckon you're another one of them damn English.' He glanced sideways at Thornton. 'What you reckon, shotgun? He an Englishman?'

Thornton remained expressionless. Had Morgan recognized him after all, and was now setting him a trap? He shrugged. 'I wouldn't know,' he said. 'Never seen an Englishman afore.'

To Thornton's relief, Morgan appeared to lose interest in the subject. Instead, he aimed his sidearm at the Englishman. 'I ain't gonna tell you agin. Send that boy over here.'

The Englishman dropped his hand from the boy's shoulder. The youngster had paled with fear, his hands by his side visibly shaking. Slowly, he began to make his way along the room towards Morgan.

'Steadfast, William,' the Englishman said.

The boy swallowed noisily. 'St-steadfast, sir,' he stammered.

'Cut the cackle!' Morgan barked. 'Git over here!'

The boy reached Morgan and stood beside him. Morgan surveyed the grim-faced men and women around the table. 'I tol' you folks there was gold on this stage.' He thrust his hand beneath his shirt and pulled out a package. 'Jed, give this to the Englishman,' he ordered. 'Blackie, go get the horses.'

'What are you doing, you blackguard?' The elderly woman who wore the gold necklace had half-risen from her seat and was staring angrily at Morgan.

'Sit down, old woman!' Morgan yelled. He swung around to face the Englishman. 'You take that package to J. T. Walker. Tell him if he wants to see his gran'son alive agin, he's gotta do what that letter says.'

130

'D'you know how many men Walker can have huntin' you?' Thornton said.

'Five hundred men cain't stop a slug goin' through this boy's head, if that's what I choose,' Morgan snarled. He looked to the doorway as horses appeared outside. 'OK, this is what we're gonna do. Hobbes is gonna ride with us for two hours. Anyone tries to follow us, we'll kill him.'

There was an anguished cry from Hobbes's wife. 'No! No!'

Morgan ignored her. 'He'll be back here in four hours, nobody gets smart.'

'If the northern stage ain't at the next station, a posse's gonna be ridin' out,' Joey French said. 'You're gonna be killin' Hobbes for the wrong reasonin'.'

Morgan frowned, appearing to think things over. 'OK, the northern stage goes on. No tricks! Remember, I got the boy.' He jerked at the boy's arm, almost pulling him over. 'Get out there, Hobbes!'

He backed away, pulling the boy the length of the table, his sidearm threatening the men and women around the table. 'You folks remember what I said you wanna see this boy alive.'

As the boy was pulled to the door, the Englishman spoke. 'Steadfast, William.'

The boy turned his face, white with fear, his eye bulging, but he managed to get his words out at the second attempt. 'Steadfast, sir.'

'Cut the cackle!'

With a final flourish of his sidearm Morgan stepped through the door. A few moments later came the sound of horses being ridden away. For several moments there was silence in the cabin, the passengers staring at each other with grim faces. Then Hobbes's wife broke the silence, speaking directly to Thornton and the Englishman.

'Please, I beg you, don't try to follow that blackguard. They will surely kill my husband.'

Thornton stepped closer to the table. He shook his head. 'We can't risk your husband or the boy,' he said. 'Morgan's a vicious killer, but he's got brains. He knows the package has to be delivered to Mr Walker.' He turned slightly. 'This gentleman will take it.'

'I'm William Frewen's tutor, his schoolmaster,' the Englishman explained. 'My name is John Hurley, from London, England.'

The elderly woman with the gold necklace spoke from the other side of the table. 'Mr Thornton, you knew that blackguard,' she said firmly. 'I saw it in your face. I'm guessing but I think you're trying to arrest him.'

'Yes, ma'am. Bart Morgan is the man who's taken the boy. I've been on his trail for several weeks.'

She nodded, as if Thornton's words were expected. Her hand strayed to the gold necklace. 'Thank you for saving my necklace, although our husbands are not senior judges.'

'No, ma'am. I guess you're the ladies of cattlemen. I reckoned that Morgan would've found that hard to deal with. Him bein' a cattle-thief.'

It was the turn of the elderly woman to look surprised. 'But how — ?'

Thornton smiled, and cut in. 'I can still hear Texas in your voice.'

The elderly woman looked at him for a moment, and then nodded. 'You're a clever man, Mr Thornton. I'm sure you'll get the boy back.'

Thornton looked around the table. 'We need to keep this to ourselves if we're goin' to get William safely home. I want you all to give me your word you'll not talk about this.'

Everyone nodded their agreement, rising from their seats and moving away from the table to prepare themselves for departure. Thornton turned to the station-keeper's wife.

'Don't worry yourself, Mrs Hobbes. I'm sure your husband will be back soon. We plan on returnin' tomorrow but one of us can stay with you if you wish.'

Her face was grim, but she shook her head. 'Me an' Hobbes fought off Comanches thirty years ago. I can wait for my man.'

'OK,' Thornton said, turning to Joey. 'You'd better get going. Shotgun here rides with you as planned. Sheriff Landon tells me that it's a quiet run from here to town.' He turned to the driver of the coach heading for town. 'You OK with me riding inside? I need to talk with Mr Hurley.'

The driver nodded. 'That's fine with me.'

'How are you going to explain being late?'

'I'll tell 'em I had to change a wheel at the station. It's happened afore.'

Twenty minutes later Joey raised his whip to Thornton in a farewell wave as the coach going north pulled away from the coach station. Thornton raised a hand in response before stepping up after Hurley to take his seat inside the stage. He thrust his head through the open space of the door.

'OK,' he called to the driver. 'Alveston, as fast as you like.'

The stage pulled away as the driver turned the heads of the lead horses in the direction of the trail. As they passed the corral Thornton caught sight of Hobbes's wife standing at the door-way, waiting. Hurley, on the opposite side of the coach, looked at Thornton with sharp, intelligent eyes.

'You seem to know what you're doing, Mr Thornton,' he said. 'But I don't see a badge. Were you a lawman?'

Thornton shook his head. 'Five years Army.' He paused, thinking. 'How well do you know J.T. Walker?'

'Not at all. I only arrived from England a few weeks ago. I've heard he's a hard man but fair. When he hears what happened he'll understand.' He paused a moment. 'But Morgan will be dead shortly,' Hurley said. His tone indicated that he'd stated a fact, rather than a wish. 'Walker will hunt him down if he has to hire a hundred men.'

'That isn't going to get the boy back alive.'

'You think Morgan would carry out his threat?'

'I'm sure of it. He slaughtered a family of homesteaders over Powder River way last summer. Then he took to thieving cattle. I've been chasin' him for weeks. If he's cornered he'll shoot the boy.' Thornton considered the options. 'Maybe two or three men would stand a chance of catching up with him and freeing the boy.'

'So we need one more.'

Thornton raised his eyebrows. 'You aimin' to be one? There's gonna be a lot of hard riding, and some shootin'.'

'I was with the 6th Regiment Bengal Cavalry for five years until I was caught in bed by my colonel.' Hurley's mouth twitched. 'I lost my commission, left India and had to leave England for a while.'

'Just for being caught in bed?'

Hurley shrugged. 'The colonel's lady was with me at the time.'

Thornton couldn't help but smile. 'OK, that's two of us. We need a tracker.'

'I've been told Landon's a good sheriff in Alveston. He may know someone.'

'We'll see him when we get to town.

Then we'll deliver the letter.'

Three hours later the stage reached Alveston. Hurley arranged for his and William's boxes to be sent out to the Bar J ranch, and then the two men walked over to the sheriff's office. Landon looked up from where he was writing at his desk as the two men stepped through the door.

'Howdy.' He glared at Thornton. 'You brought me more trouble?'

'This gentleman is Mr Hurley. He works for the boss of Powder River.'

'May we sit down, Mr Landon?' Hurley asked.

Landon waved a hand at the two chairs close to his desk. 'OK, I can see you ain't here on a social occasion. Let's hear it.'

'Bart Morgan, the man I've been chasin', is holding J.T. Walker's gran'son for ransom. Morgan took him at the stage station.'

Landon blew a silent whistle. The resigned expression on his face vanished and his mouth set in a grim line.

'Sonovabitch! You lookin' for a posse? I can get one in an hour.'

Thornton shook his head. 'Morgan's threatening to shoot the boy. Three men, keepin' low, would be better. Two of us, and we'll need a tracker.'

Landon looked at the Englishman. 'You don't mind me saying, Mr Hurley, this ain't friendly country. It's gonna be hard going.'

'I think I'll manage,' said Hurley.

'Anyone in mind for a tracker?' Thornton asked.

Landon didn't hesitate. 'Billy Three-Eyes. Useta work for the Army. Best man in this part of Wyoming.'

'Sounds like an Indian.'

Landon surprised them both with his answer. 'Depends what day it is. Might be best if I say nothing about the boy. I'll go see Billy for you. If he agrees to sign on you can brief him then.'

'Have him meet us here at dawn tomorrow,' Thornton said.

'Thank you, Mr Landon,' Hurley said, as the two men stood up. 'You've been most helpful.'

Landon looked at Thornton. 'You take Morgan alive, you bring him back here an' he goes afore a judge. This ain't Dodge City.'

'Just as you say, Mr Landon.'

* * *

Night was falling, and the shadows thrown by the two men and their horses were lengthening as they rode up to the Big House of the Bar J ranch. Hurley pointed to a large barn set maybe a hundred yards from the house.

'That looks the place for our horses tonight.'

Thornton looked across at Hurley. 'How's your mount shapin' up?'

'Very good. Butler has done well and he gave me a good deal on the saddle.'

Ten minutes later both men stepped up the broad steps to the house. Before they'd reached the boardwalk, which ran around the house, the high door was flung open, casting light around the three people who stood in the doorway.

'I guess you're John Hurley. Welcome to the Bar J.' J.T. Walker's voice was loud and warm. 'And Mr Thornton! A surprise visit, sir! I hope you've changed your mind about working for me.' Walker looked past them both, a puzzled frown on his face. 'And where's my splendid gran'son?'

'I think we should go inside, Mr Walker,' Hurley said. He gave a half-bow in the direction of the two women who stood alongside Walker. Thornton recognized one of them from the Box Social as being Walker's wife. 'Maybe the ladies will excuse us. William is not with us and I shall explain the reason.'

'What in damnation is going on?' Walker roared. 'Where's my gran'son?'

'We need to talk, Mr Walker,' Thornton said.

Walker looked at him and, appearing to recognize something in Thornton's expression, nodded abruptly and turned on his heel.

'Go into the parlour, ladies,' he said

shortly. 'We'll go into my study.'

Thornton and Hurley followed Walker down to the end of a wide corridor until they reached a door, which stood slightly ajar. Walker pushed it open and strode across the room to take his seat. He reached for a cheroot without offering one to either of the two men.

'Now tell me where my gran'son is,' he said, glaring across his desk.

In a carefully narrated sequence of events Hurley explained what had happened from the time he had innocently entered the stage station house to be confronted by Morgan until William was forced to ride away with the three men and Hobbes.

'Bart Morgan led the gang that stole cattle from Powder River,' Thornton added when Hurley had finished. 'I've taken care of the rest of the gang and was closing in on him.'

'For God's sake, Hurley! Couldn't you have stopped them?'

Thornton cut in before Hurley could reply. 'The passengers would have been killed. Mr Hurley could do nothing.'

Walker breathed in deeply before drawing heavily on his cheroot. 'What does this blackguard want? Money, I suppose.'

Hurley reached beneath his shirt and pulled out the packet given to him by Morgan. He stood up and placed it on the desk in front of Walker. The rancher looked down at it for a second before picking it up and tearing it open. There was silence in the room while Walker read through twice what appeared to be a short message. He finished reading and looked up at both men.

'Morgan wants five thousand dollars in gold for the safe return of William. I've a week to get the gold, and then I shall be sent further instructions.' He frowned. 'Who is this Morgan?'

'He's a killer with brains,' Thornton said. 'We don't want to stampede him with a big posse. But the two of us and a tracker can pick up Morgan's trail. Morgan has plenty of bluster but I reckon he could be worried. He's lost his two brothers and Darvish, the man I shot in town. The two men he has with him now aren't like the men he's lost, and they puzzle me. They're not the sort I'd expect to be riding with a man like Morgan.'

'How long d'you reckon to catch up with the sonovabitch?'

'Maybe a week, it's hard to say,' Thornton said. 'He could be circling this part of the Territory. But we don't know where he's planning to pick up the gold. We need to get close to him; we've arranged for the tracker to join us at dawn tomorrow.'

'Billy Three-Eyes is a good man,' Walker suggested.

Hurley nodded. 'He's likely to be our tracker.'

Walker looked at both men. 'I'll get word to Moreton Frewen. Bring me back my gran'son alive and kill Morgan an' you'll share the five thousand dollars.'

# 8

The rays of the early morning sun were falling along Main Street as Thornton and Hurley walked their horses from the livery, Hurley holding the rope of a pack mule behind them. Loaded on the animal were coffee and enough food for a week. Boxes contained ammunition for their sidearms and Winchesters.

The hour was too early for the townsfolk to be around but the blacksmith, busy with reviving his fire from its overnight damping, raised a hand in greeting.

Close to the hitching rail in front of the sheriff's office a tall, broad-shouldered man sat astride a big chestnut. He wore blue pants tucked into shiny leather boots, cavalry fashion, and his spurs glinted with a suggestion of silver. His woollen shirt was partly covered by a leather vest, and on his head was a clean, cream-coloured Stetson.

Thornton looked across at Hurley. 'Billy Three-Eyes, I guess. Not what I reckoned to see.'

'No, indeed.'

The two men closed the distance to the tracker, and it wasn't difficult to guess why he'd got his name. An inch above his eyebrows, in the centre of his forehead, was a scar, maybe caused by a knife. A small semi-circle bore evenly placed short vertical lines. The scar looked remarkably like a closed eye.

Thornton was even further surprised by his appearance. Bright-blue eyes showed in the man's mahogany features. 'The sheriff explained what we wanted?'

'You need a tracker. I'm the best there is. Ten years with the Army.' Billy almost smiled. 'Three-quarters Irish, a quarter Apache if you're thinkin' about where I'm from.'

Thornton stuck out his hand. 'The name's Thornton. This gentleman is Mr Hurley.'

Billy shook Thornton's hand with a firm grip and then took Hurley's outstretched hand. 'Guess you gentlemen were Army.'

Hurley looked surprised. 'How did . . . ?'

'Know the signs,' the tracker said. He turned back to Thornton. 'Thirty dollars a week, an' I'm gonna be straight. I did my time in the Army, an' I've had my fill of shootin'. I gotta beautiful woman and three sons. I wanna see the boys grow up.'

Thornton nodded. 'OK. We catch up with these no-goods an' that's your job finished.'

Billy nodded. 'It's a deal. Now, what d'you want of me?'

'I'll tell you as we go. First we need to call in at the stage station and talk to Hobbes.'

Three hours later the three men arrived at the station. Hobbes's wife, without a word of the events of the day before, served them coffee and then disappeared into the back room. Hobbes sat at the long table opposite the three men.

'I thought the sonovabitch was gonna shoot me,' he said, one hand stroking his beard. 'I gotta admit that Morgan put the fear of God into me. He went crazy when that feller with a stain on his face said it was soon gonna be time to let me loose. The other no-good saved me, tellin' Morgan you'd be on his trail if I didn't return. We got to the two-hour point an' Morgan just told me to ride back.'

'Can you tell us where they left you?'

'There's a stand o' cottonwoods with a big rock at the edge.' He shrugged his shoulders. 'I gotta be honest, I wasn't lookin' around too much. I was just glad to put distance between me and that Morgan. The way he suddenly rages makes me wonder about his mind.'

'Did you see which way they went?'

'They were still headin' north the last I seen of 'em.'

'How was the boy?' Hurley asked.

'He's a tough little feller. He didn't say a word but he looked OK.'

Thornton looked at the tracker. 'You

got any questions?'

'How big are the three men?'

'Morgan's a big sonovabitch. The other two, I guess, are built like most cowboys: medium height, wiry build.'

Billy nodded, apparently satisfied with Hobbes's answer. Thornton drained the last of his coffee. 'OK, Mr Hobbes. It's good to see you back with Mrs Hobbes. Sheriff Landon knows what's going on. J.T. Walker will speak with Warren Jenkins when he gets back to Alveston.' He stood up from the table. 'We'll be getting along.'

The three men picked up their hats and went out of the cabin to their horses. As they prepared to mount, Thornton turned to Billy. 'OK, time for hard talkin'. What are our chances?'

Billy looked thoughtful. 'The boy's gonna help us a lot,' he said after a second or two. 'If I can pick up his trail by the cottonwoods Mr Hobbes talked of, I reckon our chances are good.'

The three men trotted their horses for a few hundred yards then settled them in a lope. Billy's work would begin in a couple of hours and Thornton was keen to find out before nightfall where Morgan was heading.

* * *

Almost three hours later Thornton and Hurley were leaning against the big rock mentioned by Hobbes. Both men were smoking, Thornton drawing on a roll-up he'd built from tobacco out of the small linen bag he carried on a thin cord around his neck, and rolled in brown paper that he'd found in a vest pocket. Not for the first time did he regret the Bull Durham people ceasing to attach papers to the bag of tobacco.

Hurley was puffing away on a curved pipe. For almost half an hour they had watched Billy walk slowly backwards and forwards in front of them. Now he was several hundred yards along the trail.

'You reckon he'll find — ' Hurley broke off, as with a whoop of triumph

Billy whirled around and held up his arm. 'OK, I see it,' the tracker called.

'How the hell does he do that?' Thornton said, extinguishing his smoke as Hurley banged his pipe against the heel of his boot. Both men walked quickly to where their horses were loosely tethered to one of the cottonwoods. Thornton mounted, and leaned down to free Billy's horse, turning the animal's head to guide it to the tracker.

'Tol' you the boy would be the answer,' Billy said when they reached him. He pointed to the ground. 'See how the buffalo grass ain't bent over so much?'

Thornton looked down, before glancing across at Hurley. 'I'm gonna take your word for it, Billy. I reckon you've already earned your thirty dollars.'

'We're just starting,' Billy said. 'But if they stay on this trail we could find 'em in the next settlement we reach.'

'Morgan's too smart for that. Somewhere along this trail he's gonna break east or west.'

'I don't see him goin' east. There's nothin' out there but rocks and dirt and water's hard to find.'

'So what we got over to the west?'

'We got a problem, that's what. There's half a dozen settlements strung out. Each one mebbe a coupla days' ride off this trail. Even when I see Morgan break from the trail I'll not be sure which settlement they're heading for. The trail to the west of here is used by lots of folk, wagons an' stuff.' The tracker looked to the north. 'I'll take some grub an' get ahead of you. If I lose 'em and need to come back you'll not waste any time.'

'OK, we'll stay on the trail so we'll be easy to find.'

The tracker, having pushed a bag of biscuits into his saddle-bag and checked he had water, gave the two men a brief nod and kicked his horse forward in a smart trot. Thornton and Hurley remained silent for a few moments as they watched him go.

'Billy doesn't find the trail we're

gonna be checkin' a lot of places,' Thornton said slowly. 'I hope to hell Morgan hasn't already planned a hideout.'

'Maybe we should have let Mr Walker put together a big posse.'

Thornton shook his head. 'They'd have stampeded Morgan into getting rid of the boy, an' that's if they could have found him. I'm backing Billy to lead us to him.'

The two men kicked their horses forward, staying close enough to be able to talk comfortably. Ahead of them, Billy was slowly moving further away, appearing to be confident that he was following Morgan's trail.

'What puzzles me,' Thornton said, 'is Morgan's mention of further instructions. Does he have someone in town workin' with him?'

'Maybe this is a wild-goose chase and he's circling to return close to Alveston. Could we take a gamble and return to town?'

'There are too many places 'round

Alveston he could hole up,' Thornton said. 'We could take a year an' never find him. No, I reckon we stay on his trail and plan to come up on him. Then even if he does go back to Alveston we'll have some notion where he's to be found.'

Hurley started to reply but then stood up in his stirrups and looked ahead in Billy's direction. 'I reckon Billy's found something.'

Thornton looked to see the tracker, his hat in hand, waving furiously at them. Both men dug their heels into the sides of their animals and rode fast to where the tracker, a big grin on his face, was pointing westwards.

'They left the trail here. It ain't over fer us yet cos of all the settlements, but there's a wagon over by the water. Folks in the wagon might have seen them ridin' through.'

Thornton looked in the direction of where Billy was pointing. His eyes followed the course of the water, more a generous stream than a small river, but he could see nothing of a wagon. He turned to Hurley. 'You see the wagon?'

Hurley shook his head. Thornton leaned back to plunge his hand into his saddle-bag, pulling out a battered brass spyglass. He raised it to his eye, turning the barrel to shift focus, and moving the spyglass to follow the bend of the waterway. A stand of trees came into his view, and by the edge of the trees stood a wagon, its grey-white canvas a smudge against the green.

'OK, I see it,' Thornton said. He handed the spyglass to Hurley, who, similarly, raised it to his eye, twisting the barrel to adjust the focus to his own liking.

'You reckon Morgan's following the river?' Thornton asked Billy.

'Reckon so, it makes sense. It'll lead him to the trail that runs past the settlements. He's got a choice then between half a dozen places to hole up.'

Thornton breathed in. 'Sonovabitch must have a hideout some place. These settlements got any law?'

'They ain't bad places if that's what you mean. A couple of 'em even gotta sheriff.'

'OK, we'll go an' ask the folks on the wagon if they saw anythin'.' He made to leave, but then looked back at Billy. 'Just how far can you see?'

The tracker grinned. 'A long way,' he said.

Thornton turned the head of his mount. With luck the wagon had been travelling east, maybe planning to call in at Alveston. A single wagon was unlikely to be carrying folks planning a new life. Pioneers would be travelling westwards, so the wagon was probably being driven by folks who lived not far away. In that case, knowing the Territory, they might have a rough guess where Morgan was heading for, if by chance they'd come across him. He kicked his horse forward.

'I'm gonna catch up with you, Morgan, you sonovabitch,' he said out loud.

★　★　★

Two hours later the three men were a few hundred yards from the Conestoga wagon where it stood in the shadows of the cottonwoods. The only sound, aside from the breathing of the three horses, and the creak of leather as the men shifted in their saddles, was the splashing of water over stones in the nearby creek. Nobody appeared to greet them and there were no other signs of life. The three men reined in and sat looking ahead.

'Are we riding into a trap?' Hurley said quietly.

'Let's find out,' Thornton said. He reached down to unsheathe his Winchester from its scabbard. Levering a slug ready to fire, he raised the long gun. 'Any shootin' an' we split up. Billy, you go right; Hurley, go left.'

Taking careful aim a few feet above the canvas of the wagon, he fired. There was a whoosh of leaves being shredded but then silence. Thornton sat there, watching intently. Nothing moved. Two minutes passed; the three men sat, staring at the wagon. Thornton sheathed his Winchester and drew his Colt.

'You two stay here,' he ordered. 'I'm gonna take a look.'

He walked his horse slowly towards the wagon. One hand held the reins, the other held his Colt loosely by his side. His head turned from side to side, taking in the surroundings. It wasn't unknown to see a solitary wagon making its way across the Territory — he and Macrae back at Powder River had come across more than one — but it was unusual to see one abandoned, if that's what he was about to discover. Morgan wouldn't have let him get this close, of that he was sure. But that didn't mean other no-goods weren't around.

He saw that a pair of horses stood in the shafts of the Conestoga. This was no pioneer's wagon. Its load would be far lighter than the three or four tons the wagon could carry when pulled by oxen. He was fifty yards from the wagon when he neck-reined his mount and rode in a semi-circle. Then, as the other side of the wagon came into view his muscles unclenched. Paint, on the side of the canvas, announced the sale of household goods. Tacked to the wagon boards by long nails hung a line of pots and pans, all ready to be sold.

He urged his mount forward, covering the few yards to enable him to peer into the interior of the wagon. He saw a pile of blankets, folded on a board, opposite rough wooden shelves, which held boxes, presumably of food. An open box full of tools stood in one corner. On the floor of the wagon lay a shovel leaning against a saddle. Thornton turned to call to the others. That was when he saw the grave. Ten yards beyond the wagon, close to the cottonwoods, a mound of earth was marked with a rough wooden cross.

Thornton raised an arm. 'OK, all clear,' he called to the others.

Hurley reached him first, looking to where Thornton was pointing. 'He didn't bury himself,' Thornton said. 'But why would anyone abandon a wagon?'

'Cholera, maybe?' Hurley said grimly.

'For Chris'sakes, I hope not. I reckon they'd have burned the wagon had it been cholera.'

Billy joined them. 'I've taken a look at the horses. They're fed an' watered so folks are still around here or they ain't been gone a long time.'

The three men dismounted. 'We'll take a quick look just in case anyone's hurt an' needs help, but I don't want to get too far behind Morgan,' Thornton said. 'Take a look in the wagon, Billy. See if you get any notion of what's been goin' on.'

Billy put a foot up to enter the wagon when a shrill voice rang out from somewhere behind them. 'Don't you steal anything!'

The three men turned. Walking towards them through a gap in the cottonwoods was a young woman. Her hand was extended and the pistol she was holding was aimed at Thornton. He

160

exchanged a quick glance with Hurley, who'd been looking at her with an expression of amazement.

'Ma'am, we're righteous men and we mean you no harm,' Thornton called out. 'I reckon you should put that pistol down. If I'm right it's an old French Mariette. That makes it about fifty years old. You pull the trigger an' it's likely to blow your hand off.'

The young woman, who wore a long blue woollen skirt topped with a grey cotton blouse and a woollen vest, looked down at the pistol and then back up to Thornton, her grey eyes showing anger. 'You're trying to trick me! All three of you get away from that wagon. I'm warning you!'

Thornton stepped forward. 'We mean you no harm, ma'am. Please don't pull that trigger. You could lose your hand.' And maybe kill me in the process, he thought, keeping the friendly smile on his face. Taking slow steps, he advanced on the woman until he was only a couple of feet away. Very slowly, he raised his hand and reached out for the pistol.

'Get back, I told you!'

Thornton dropped his hand to his side. 'Did you bury the wagoner?'

She nodded abruptly, her eyes blurring. 'The brute never gave Mr Wilkins a chance.'

'Was the no-good a big man, wearing a woollen coat and a blue hat?'

Her eyes widened. 'Yes.' She bent her head suddenly, her arm dropping by her side. Tears ran down her face. 'Mr Wilkins was such a gentle old man,' she said.

Thornton reached forward and gently laid his hand on the pistol. For a second the young woman's fingers remained tightly curled around the butt. Then she relaxed and allowed Thornton to take it from her. He glanced down. As he'd guessed, it was a Mariette. The colour of the metal showed it hadn't been cleaned in a very long time. He hadn't been wrong when he'd told her that she could lose her hand.

'C'mon an' meet my friends,' he said. 'Then tell us what happened.'

She nodded, wiping her cheeks with a small square of lace. 'Thank you. I thought the Territory was safe now. All those hold-up men and thieves were long gone, I'd been told. Then those dreadful men arrived.' She looked puzzled for a moment. 'There was a boy with them.'

'I'll explain,' Thornton said.

He introduced the two others, both of whom tugged at the brims of their hats and expressed their sympathy. The young woman looked at Hurley. 'Are you English?'

'Yes, I am.'

'I spent a year in England,' she explained. 'My name is Amanda Greeley.'

'So how d'you end up with a drummer selling pots and pans?' Thornton asked.

'I ran out of money,' Amanda said frankly. 'I have to get to Cheyenne, and Mr Wilkins,' she paused to dab the lace to an eye, 'Mr Wilkins agreed to take me.'

'And you without money?' Billy said.
'He loved music, he told me.'

Although puzzled by her answer, Thornton let it go. 'Tell me what happened?'

'Mr Wilkins and I spent the night here. The next morning, that would be yesterday, I was down at the water washing when I heard riders arrive. I didn't pay them much notice, and I was only wearing a shift so I kept quiet and out of sight. I heard the men's voices, and then Mr Wilkins protesting.'

'What were the men trying to do?'

'Mr Wilkins had some bottles of whiskey and I think the men were trying to steal them. The big man in the blue hat was speaking quite calmly, and then suddenly he seemed to explode. He took hold of Mr Wilkins by his throat and shook him. Then he pushed Mr Wilkins away, pulled out his gun and shot him.' She turned away from the three men and raised the lace to her face, before turning back. 'The men rode away, that's when I saw the boy.

But I was frightened they'd come back and I stayed among the trees until nightfall. Poor Mr Wilkins stayed on the ground all night covered in one of his blankets but then I buried him at first light this morning.'

'We know who the men are,' Thornton said. 'We know they're heading west. They'll pay for what they did here.' He thought for a moment. 'You can take the wagon or you can take one of the wagon horses and ride east to Alveston. It's quite safe.'

'Ride to the Bar J,' Hurley said. 'Tell them I sent you.'

Thornton was surprised to see the young woman shake her head. 'I can't do that. I have to get to Cheyenne.'

'The Bar J will take care of you,' Hurley said. 'I promise.'

'Thank you, but I have to get to Cheyenne.'

'Are you getting married?' Billy asked.

For the first time since the young woman had appeared, the three men saw her face clear, and she laughed. Thornton couldn't help thinking it was like the sound of tinkling bells.

'No, I'm aiming to join the new orchestra they're planning. I'll ride one of the wagon horses and the other as a pack horse. As you're riding west I'll ride with you.'

'We can't allow that, ma'am,' Thornton said firmly. 'We're tracking those no-goods who were here. They could be heading anywhere. You ride to the Bar J like Mr Hurley says.'

'But it makes good sense for me to ride with you.'

The three men exchanged glances. 'Give me one good reason why it makes sense,' Thornton said shortly.

Amanda looked around. 'Because I know where the men you are chasing are going,' she said sweetly.

# 9

For almost an hour Thornton and Hurley tried to persuade Amanda to tell them what she'd heard. She sat on a fallen tree trunk, shaking her head in response to Thornton's every question and insisting she ride west with the three men.

'I'm not heartless, Mr Thornton, but I have to get to Cheyenne as soon as possible. I know you need to save the boy but I'll not be a burden and after two or three days I'll be gone.'

Finally Thornton, his face reddening with frustration, left further questioning to Hurley, hoping that his gentle English manners would talk her into telling them what she knew.

'Explain to this young woman what will happen to William if we don't catch up with Morgan.'

Hurley spoke in a soft voice, a kind

smile on his face, prompting Thornton to wonder what he was really thinking, knowing that it was likely Walker would hold him responsible for the boy's safety.

'Miss Amanda, you've seen how vicious these men are. Unless we stop them they will kill the boy,' Hurley said. 'If they learn we're on their trail they could stand and fight. Ignore these foolish stories they have back East; there is nothing heroic about fighting with guns. These men will sneak up while we sleep and try to kill us. They'll not spare you. Please tell us where the men are going and then ride to the Bar J. Mr Walker will see you're safe until we return.'

Amanda shook her head. 'You gentlemen are my chance to safely reach Cheyenne without delay. I'm riding west with you.'

Finally, she pressed her lips together with the obvious intention of not saying another word.

'Miss Amanda, I've a good mind to

put you across my — '

Her eyes flashed, her face turning pink. 'Don't you dare!'

Thornton was unable to restrain a laugh. He got to his feet from where he'd been squatting on the ground. 'OK, Miss Amanda. You win,' he said. 'Choose one of the wagon horses to ride and the other can be a pack horse.'

'Mr Wilkins told me he often rode the chestnut. He's a good strong horse.'

'Fine. D'you have much to take with you?'

'There's food from the wagon, my bits and bobs and my violin.'

A violin? The three men exchanged glances. 'For thirty a week this is sure interesting,' Billy said, a big grin splitting his face.

Thornton looked up at the sky. 'Best we stay here for the night. You can sleep in the wagon, Miss Amanda, and we'll put our blankets down by the fire.'

★　★　★

Dawn was breaking as Thornton walked back from the river, scrubbing at his face and hands with the rough cloth he'd taken from his saddle-bag. The other two men were rolling up their blankets, preparing to tie them to their saddles.

Thornton looked across to the wagon where the canvas was still secured with lashings. 'You go down to the river,' he ordered the two men. 'Do what you gotta do an' be as quick about it as you can.' He kicked at the embers of the fire, stirring flames from the kindling the three had kept burning during the night. 'I'll brew coffee an' get Miss Amanda up.'

As Billy and Hurley finished securing their blankets and walked through the cottonwoods Thornton crossed to the wagon and rapped on the board. 'Time you were shiftin', Miss Amanda,' he called.

He stepped back a few feet when he heard sounds of movement from within the wagon. Amanda's head appeared, thrust through a gap in the canvas.

'Billy an' Mr Hurley are down at the river. When they come back you can go down there. Don't take too long as we need to get on the trail.'

Amanda put her hand to her mouth to cover a yawn. 'I'll be there, Mr Thornton.'

'Get your stuff together, an' we'll load it on the pack horse.' He looked directly at her. 'Get one thing straight. You hold us up an' we'll cut you loose.'

Amanda's hand dropped and her mouth set in a determined line. 'I'll not hold you up,' she said, and disappeared behind the canvas.

'Then I sure hope you can ride that chestnut or you're takin' the wagon to the Bar J,' he called out, but there was no reply.

An hour later when he saw Amanda step up to the chestnut he had to admit that she certainly looked as if she could ride the animal. Bunching her ankle-length skirt in one hand she threw a leg across the horse and settled herself in the saddle. Thornton couldn't resist remarking on his surprise.

'Workin' gals fork a horse. I don't remember seein' a lady ride thataways.'

'It's a long story, Mr Thornton.' Amanda looked over her shoulder. 'What will happen to the wagon?'

'Wilkins have any kinfolk?'

'Only a cousin, I think. Poor Mr Wilkins was a solitary man.'

'We'll report it in the next town.' Thornton looked around at his companions. 'OK, let's ride an' catch up with Morgan.'

\* \* \*

Throughout the morning Thornton kept his mount at a steady lope, Billy alongside him, Hurley and Amanda riding close behind. Every couple of miles or so Billy briefly broke away from the others to check they were still following Morgan's tracks. At midday they rested their horses, allowing the animals to drink briefly from a nearby creek.

'We'll not catch up afore nightfall,' Billy told Thornton as the four drank from their canteens and chewed on cuts of pemmican.

'OK, we'll keep ridin' an' make camp overnight,' Thornton said. 'Tomorrow the horses will be fresh an' we'll be sharper after a night's sleep.'

As the light began to fade Thornton called a halt. Each man took care of his own horse and Hurley helped settle Amanda's chestnut. The pack horses were unloaded and hobbled. All four filled their canteens from the river, and then Billy got a fire going for coffee. Amanda searched among her food stores and found two cans of peaches and a can of beef. An hour after they'd pitched camp they were sitting on their blankets around a blazing fire.

'Sure beats the pemmican, Miss Amanda,' Billy said as he speared a slice of peach with his knife. He looked across the fire to Thornton. 'We're gonna meet the north-south trail tomorrow. Mebbe around noon.'

Thornton nodded and looked across at Amanda. 'I'm gonna turn in,' was all he said.

★ ★ ★

The sun was high in the sky the following day when Billy Three-Eyes stood up in his stirrups and pointed ahead. 'That's where the trail breaks just beyond that old cabin,' he said. 'I ain't promisin' I'm gonna find their tracks. Mr Thornton, you gotta decide. We going north or south?'

Thornton drew his mount alongside Amanda. 'Time to tell us what you know, Miss Amanda. A boy's life depends on it.'

'Willings Ferry,' she said. 'I heard the man in the blue hat say that's where they needed to be.'

Thornton frowned. 'Did he give any reason?'

Amanda shook her head.

Thornton turned to Billy. 'You know the place?'

'Sure do. We're in luck. Willings is the

first settlement south. It's a righteous place. There's a sheriff, coupla boardin' houses I know well, an' a respectable hotel.'

'Billy, you go to the boardin' house. See us tomorrow an' I'll pay you off. Miss Amanda, you can ride to Cheyenne after you've rested. I'll spring for your hotel room.' He smiled. 'You can play some music an' pay me back.'

'S'posin' Morgan's at the hotel?' Billy said.

Thornton's mouth twitched. 'Then we'll not need to go lookin' for him.'

'I've an idea for Miss Amanda,' Hurley said. 'Billy, I'll give you twenty dollars to see Miss Amanda safely to Cheyenne.'

A big grin showed on the tracker's face. 'I sure do like ridin' with you gentlemen,' Billy said. 'Suits me fine, if that sets OK with Miss Amanda.'

'That's wonderful!' Amanda's face, too, was wreathed with smiles. 'I'll pay back the twenty dollars, Mr Hurley. I promise.'

'OK. That's all fixed,' Thornton said. He turned his horse's head. 'Now let's go get the boy. What the hell — ?' he shouted as his mount threw its head back in fear.

Amanda shrieked. Blood spurted from the neck of her horse, as the sound of a long gun reached them. She was thrown to the ground as her mount toppled sideways, blood coming from its nostrils, drops spattering the hem of Amanda's skirts. The momentum of her fall sent her rolling across the buffalo grass.

Billy, knife in hand, slashed through the lead rein of Amanda's pack horse.

'Make for the trees!' Thornton yelled.

Both he and Hurley rode either side of Amanda, each leaning from the saddle to grab an arm and hoisting her between the two horses. Another two shots rang out, the air buzzing close to Thornton's head. Bent low, the three men kicked their horses forward, Amanda squealing with fear, her button shoes scraping the buffalo grass before she was able to kick clear of the ground.

The air was tearing at Thornton's lungs as he and Hurley reached the protection of the stand of cottonwoods bordering the river, Billy Three-Eyes close behind. They weaved through the trees, heads down to avoid the low-hanging branches, and halted their mounts in a clearing, allowing Amanda to drop to the ground. All three men stood down from their saddles, Amanda dropping to her knees, her head down, her throat bobbling with stifled gulps.

Through a gap in the trees Thornton could see Amanda's pack horse, alarmed by the shooting, running towards the higher ground. A shot rang out and blood spurted from the animal's head. With a tortured scream of agony the horse fell to the ground, quivered, and then was still.

'They've shot Amanda's pack horse,' Thornton said grimly.

Amanda pushed around, still on her knees on the ground. 'Oh, my God! My violin!'

'Sonovabitch!' Thornton swore. 'Did you see where they're holed up?'

'In that old cabin, I reckon,' Hurley said. He looked down at Amanda, clambering to her knees. 'We'll get your violin back, Miss Amanda,' he said.

She looked up at the Englishman, her face white, her eyes wide with shock. 'Oh, please! Please! I must have my violin.'

'Let's take a look,' Thornton said. 'Billy, you stay here and look after Miss Amanda.'

'Sure thing, boss.'

Thornton and Hurley made their way to the outer ring of trees. Both men carried a Winchester, and Thornton had his Navy Colt by his side. 'Morgan's smart,' Thornton said. 'He must have known we were tracking him. How many, d'you reckon?'

'No more than two.'

Both men, treading cautiously, moved from tree to tree, until they could see the ground surrounding the old cabin. A few yards from its door a long-abandoned wagon was on its side, two of its wheels in the air, their rims hanging loosely from wooden spokes. A pile of straw bales, once the wagon's load, but now rotted by weather and time, was scattered on the ground.

'High ground on our left,' Hurley said. 'If one of us could reach it there'd be a line of fire down to the cabin.'

'An' the other gets to the wagon,' Thornton said.

'You reckon it's worth trying?'

'Those coupla no-goods can sit there makin' sure we never catch up with Morgan. We gotta try it.' Thornton pulled up the corner of his mouth. 'Mebbe we shoulda both stuck to the Army — it was safer.'

Hurley smiled grimly. 'We've got the sun behind us.'

Thornton nodded. 'Let's get our horses.'

Back in the clearing Thornton stepped up to his saddle. He looked down at Billy. 'S'posin' we don't come back.'

'Miss Amanda an' me can swim. We get across the river an' I can hold off two no-goods for as long as it takes.'

Hurley looked down at Amanda, her pale face tilted to look up at the Englishman. 'Miss Amanda, don't you concern yourself. Mr Thornton and I are coming back and I'll have your violin.'

'Take care, both of you.'

Both men turned their horses' heads and walked their animals to a small clear patch at the edge of the cotton-woods. 'We gotta come outta these trees at a pace, I reckon,' Thornton said. 'There's a chance we'll catch those no-goods won-derin' what we're up to.'

Both men lined up their mounts, put-ting several yards between the horses to provide separate targets when they burst out into the open. 'Hurley, you ready?'

The Englishman's mouth was set. 'Steadfast,' he said.

With a deep-throated shout Thornton dug his spurs into the sides of his horse and broke from the shelter of the trees.

He was low in the saddle over the neck of his horse, vaguely aware that Hurley was already twenty yards from him, heading for the higher ground. Dirt kicked up a few yards from his horse's hoofs as from the cabin came the sounds of long guns firing rapidly. The muscles in Thornton's gut tightened as he realized the men in the cabin were armed with Winchesters. The broken wagon seemed a mile away.

He neck-reined his horse, veering to the right, his heart feeling as if it would burst from its cage. Maybe fifty yards to the wagon, he reckoned. He pulled around the horse's head once more as the air buzzed around him with slugs from one of the Winchesters. Twenty yards to the wagon. He urged his horse on, the animal's breath clouding the air. Ten yards. Five yards.

He snatched at his Winchester, kicked away his irons and rolled from his saddle, hitting the ground hard, the air rushing from his lungs. His Navy Colt bit into his hip and he cursed aloud. His Winchester slammed against the rock-hard ground and was torn from his gasp, flying through the air.

He rolled across the ground the two or three yards to the shelter of the wagon. He looked behind him for his long gun but there was no way he could reach his Winchester without exposing himself to the men who could not fail to miss. From now on he would have to depend on his Navy Colt.

He twisted his head around to search for Hurley. A hundred yards away, Hurley's horse was free, trotting back to the stand of cottonwoods, Thornton's roan close behind. Had the Englishman been hit? Then, from behind a fallen log a hat was waved, followed by more shots from the cabin. Relieved to see that Hurley had made it to safety, Thornton blew out air between pursed lips.

Straw flew into the air above his head as shots rang out from the interior of the cabin, the slugs hammering into the bales of the abandoned wagon load. He pushed himself up on one knee and scrabbled along the length of the wagon to peer between the split planks. The shutter of the cabin had been pushed open and in the gap two men stood alongside each other, their long guns held to their shoulders, one man aiming at the high ground where he thought Hurley was sheltering, the other swinging his Winchester to aim first at the high ground then in the direction of the wagon.

Thornton calculated it was maybe twenty yards to the cabin from the wagon, twice the range that he could be sure of hitting the pair with his sidearm. The ground was flat and firm but Thornton knew if he attempted to close the range he was faced with the longest run of his life, and the odds were against him making it. Hurley had said he was good with a long gun. If ever there was a time for the Englishman to back up his claim, this was it. Thornton shifted from his knee to a crouch, ready to take off when the time was right. He held his arm outstretched at shoulder level in the prearranged signal.

From the high ground came a volley of shots, the air humming as Hurley poured fire on the open shutter of the cabin. The constant levering of the Englishman's Winchester seemed to Thornton almost as if a Gatling was firing. Christ! The Englishman could handle a long gun.

There was a cry of pain as one of the men staggered back, cursing. Now! Thornton launched himself from behind the wagon, sucking air into his lungs, his Navy held in his outstretched arm. He raced across the ground, willing himself not to pull the trigger and waste valuable lead. He saw the one remaining rifle swing around, light flashing on the barrel from the midday sun. The streak of pain across his gut told him he was at the very edge of the range he knew he could hit his target. As he heard the ratchet grind of the man reloading he pulled the trigger of his Navy, his arm held high and outstretched as he used the sidearm's sight to concentrate his aim.

A red bloom appeared on the rifleman's face and he was thrown back inside the cabin. Thornton kept on running to the gap in the cabin, his Navy held out ready to fire. In the shadows of the cabin two men lay on the ground. Were they both dead? Always check. He moved quickly, pushing through the door of the cabin. The bushwhacker he'd hit with his Navy was on his back, sightless eyes staring upwards; but the other was still alive. Thornton moved to the one in the corner and looked down. Blood had spattered his red hair. His eyes glowed with hatred. Lips pulled back from tobacco-stained teeth.

'Morgan will kill . . . '

His head fell back, and Thornton lowered his Navy. The man was dead.

He turned as Hurley burst through the door, his sidearm held high. The Englishman stopped as he surveyed the inside of the cabin. He managed a strained smile, poking a finger through the hole in the brim of his hat.

'One of these fellers got damned close,' he said ruefully.

Thornton frowned as a thought came to him. 'How did these two men know we were trackin' Morgan? We coulda been regular townsfolk ridin' to one o' the settlements.'

'You think we were seen leaving Alveston?'

'Mebbe so.' He looked down at the bodies. 'I ain't seen 'em afore. Mebbe Morgan hired 'em in Willings Ferry.'

'Or maybe they were there waiting for him,' Hurley suggested.

'Yeah, could be. We'll let the sheriff know what's gone on. Mebbe he'll know if Morgan's in town. You'd best rescue Miss Amanda's violin.'

* * *

Three hours later the four riders reined in outside the sheriff's office at Willings Ferry. Hurley had Amanda's two carpet bags lashed to his saddle, while Amanda, astride the second wagon horse, clutched at her violin case. Daylight was beginning to fade and through the window of the office Thornton could see a yellow lamp throwing shadows across a tall man leaning over his desk, shuffling through papers. Thornton stepped down from his horse.

'Stay here. I'll not be long.'

He went up the steps to the boardwalk and pushed through the door. The pot-bellied stove in the corner of the office provided a pleasant warmth for the cool evening. The tall man, a star on his chest, turned from the desk to face Thornton, sharp eyes weighing him up.

'Howdy, stranger.'

Thornton glanced at the nameboard on the side of the desk. 'Howdy, Sheriff Gleason. The name's Thornton. There are two men dead in a cabin close to where the trail from the east joins the trail leadin' here. They tried to bushwhack four of us, includin' a gentlewoman.'

The sheriff's eyes dropped to Thornton's Colt. 'You chased 'em off all on your own?'

Thornton shook his head. 'There's an Englishman outside, mighty handy with a long gun.'

'What did these men look like?'

Thornton thought for a moment. 'One of 'em had black hair an' a ring in his ear.'

It was Gleason's turn to think for a few seconds. Then he walked across the office and picked up a thick volume. He brought it back to his desk and flicked through the pages. Finally, he stopped and pushed the volume across the desk towards Thornton.

'This the critter?'

Thornton looked down at the artist's sketch of a man's head below the large black letters, which spelt out: 'Wanted for Murder'.

He nodded. 'That's the no-good.'

The sheriff flicked over more pages. 'Chavez rides with another no-good by the name of Hooley.' He found another wanted notice. 'That him?'

'That's the sonovabitch.'

'You wanna ride to Alveston you got yourself a reward. Sheriff Landon's been lookin' fer these two for a year or more.'

'You heard of a feller name o' Bart Morgan?'

The sheriff shook his head. 'Nope.'

'He wears an unusual hat. Blue Dakota, same style as my Stetson, only it's got a whipped brim.'

Again Gleason shook his head. 'No, cain't say I — ' He broke off, thinking, then he nodded. 'Yeah, I coulda done. Saw a feller with a hat like that when he rode into town a coupla days back. Had a boy an' a coupla cowboys with him.'

'He still in town?'

The sheriff shrugged. 'I ain't seen him since. But that don't mean nothin' if he ain't been causin' me trouble.'

'He's trouble, Mr Gleason. I've been trackin' him since a while back.'

'What's he done?'

'Stolen a boy.'

The sheriff's mouth set. 'The boy I coulda seen him with?'

'I reckon so. We're gonna be lookin' for him but I'm guessin' he's already moved on. I'll let you know if I do find him still in town.'

* * *

Thornton and his companions reined in outside the Huntsman's Hotel as the glow from a dozen or more lamps splashed light on to the hardpack along Main Street. Storekeepers were closing their shutters, the thud of wood meeting wood sounding along the street.

'I'm gonna find the boarding house,' Billy announced. 'Coupla fellers live there I ain't seen for a year or more. It's a good chance to catch up with 'em and hear their news.'

'OK. Meet Miss Amanda tomorrow morning. You'll get your money then.'

'Sure thing, Mr Thornton.' For a moment Billy looked along the street avoiding Thornton's steady gaze. 'You ain't thinkin' bad o' me cos I didn't stand with you today?'

Thornton shook his head. 'We made a deal, Billy, and you were straight. You've a family. Me an' Mr Hurley, we don't have fine boys an' a wife to go back to.'

Reassured, Billy touched the brim of his hat and turned the head of his horse. Thornton watched him go. 'He's a good man,' he said to Hurley and Amanda. Then he stepped down from his horse. 'Let's see if they have room for us.'

Inside, the hotel was much as Thornton expected. A floor of painted boards covered in some places with rugs. Around the space in front of the desk were scattered a few low tables and some horsehair sofas and chairs. On the walls were hung dark paintings of cowboys chasing steers.

'Evenin' ma'am, gentlemen.'

The clerk was a young man in his twenties, dressed in a grey city suit, a stiff collar at his throat adorned with a blue tie boasting a knot almost as big as a breakfast biscuit.

'Three rooms, if you have them?' Thornton said.

'You're in luck, sir. Gentleman an' his wife an' son left coupla days ago. A dollar a night, and breakfast for fifty cents across at the Chinaman's place.'

'OK, we'll take them.'

The young man looked around at the three, and appeared to reach a decision. 'Pay when you leave, sir. I'll have someone walk your horses to the livery.' He gave an apologetic smile. 'Sheriff Gleason requires you to leave your weapons with me while you're in the hotel.'

'We'll get our saddle-bags an' be back. We've a pack mule with us. The livery in town OK?'

'Belton's an honest man, sir. Your rig will be safe. I'll show the lady to her room.' He glanced at the violin case carried by Amanda and then turned aside to call through the doorway of a room at the rear of the desk. 'Jed, give a hand with the lady's bags, and then take the horses to the livery.' He looked at Amanda. 'I'll carry the case for you, ma'am.'

Amanda smiled. 'That's courteous but I'll carry it myself. It's not heavy.'

A few minutes later Thornton and Hurley re-entered the hotel, saddle-bags over their shoulders, Winchester rifles held loosely, each man carrying one of Amanda's carpet bags. They handed them over as the clerk again took his place behind the desk. A thought came to Thornton as he and Hurley then handed over their Winchesters.

'I don't s'pose you've seen a feller in town favourin' a blue hat somethin' like mine?'

'Why yes! Mr Morgan was a guest. He was the man with his wife and boy who left yesterday. His two companions are still upstairs.'

Thornton kept his voice even. 'One with a stain on the side of his face?'

'Sure. That's Mr Wilson. He and Mr Reese are in room four.'

Thornton exchanged glances with Hurley. Both men put their saddle-bags on the counter and together they turned towards the staircase leading to the rooms upstairs.

The clerk coughed loudly. 'Gentlemen, your sidearms!'

Thornton turned back, thrusting a hand into his vest pocket and pulling out a coin. He put it on the counter. The clerk gazed down at the profile of the woman wearing a turban on her head above the figures '1798'. He reached forward slowly to turn over the coin and with his mouth half open stared at the engraving of the giant bird.

'Is that a half eagle? I've never seen one before,' he said slowly.

Thornton nodded. 'Five dollars. They're yourn.'

The clerk looked at the two men in turn, seemingly torn between accepting the five dollars and his duty. Then he gave a brief nod. 'Please, no killin's,' he pleaded. 'Sheriff Gleason will run me out of town.'

Thornton settled his Navy on his hip. 'You ready, Mr Hurley?'

# 10

Thornton and Hurley stepped cautiously along the uncarpeted boards of the corridor leading to the room of the two men they'd last seen when William was taken by Morgan. Thornton held his sidearm half-raised, ready if either Wilson or Reese suddenly appeared. They reached the room, Thornton putting his ear close to the door. From inside came the clink of glasses and the fluttering whisper of cards being dealt. Thornton heard one of the men speak.

'My luck's gonna change, I know it.'

Thornton stood back and nodded at Hurley, who stepped forward and rapped on the door. 'Mr Wilson,' he called. 'Message for you.'

There was a pause and then from behind the door came the sound of a chair being pushed back along boards. 'OK, comin'.'

Thornton raised his Colt as Hurley stood back. The door opened.

'Yeah, who — ?'

Wilson froze in the doorway as the muzzle of Thornton's Navy was pressed against his nose. 'Back up,' Thornton ordered. 'If Reese reaches for a gun, you die now.'

Wilson took a step back, his expression taut. 'We ain't got guns. I swear it!'

'Keep backin',' Thornton barked. 'Reese, move to the bed an' keep your hands where we can see 'em. He makes a move, Mr Hurley, shoot him.'

'Fer Chris'sakes don't kill us. We ain't done nothin',' Reese croaked. 'We jest want all this finished.'

Thornton ignored him. He pushed his Colt harder against Wilson's nose. 'You get with Reese. We got some questions afore Sheriff Gleason throws you in jail.'

He watched both men carefully as Wilson backed away to sit alongside Reese on the bed. Thornton checked that Hurley had his sidearm in his hand, and slid his Navy back into its holster. He picked up one of the cane chairs from beside the small table on which cards were scattered. He swung it around and straddled the chair, staring hard at the two men.

'I'm gonna ask some questions. You're both in fer a beatin' if you lie. You got that?'

Both men nodded furiously and Thornton frowned. He'd expected resistance, even an attempt to come at him with a knife if their sidearms were down below with the clerk. But the two men seemed almost too anxious to please.

'Where's the boy?'

'Morgan took him yesterday. He an' a woman. That's the reason we came here. So she could join him.'

'She Morgan's woman?'

'I reckon,' Reese said. 'But she ain't like Morgan. No, sir. She ain't got no notion that Morgan's taken the boy. Morgan said he'd kill us if we said anythin' to her. Same with the boy.'

'How is William?'

'He's damned scared. But he's a brave little critter.' Reese looked at Wilson. 'What's that word, he useta say?'

'Steadsomethin',' Wilson said.

'Steadfast,' Hurley said from behind Thornton.

Wilson looked up. 'Yeah, that's it.'

Thornton looked at both men in turn. There was something wrong here. 'What the hell you two doin' ridin' with a man like Morgan?'

'We had to,' said Reese heavily. 'We got into a fight in a saloon over to the west of the Territory. Sheriff threw us in jail for the night. Morgan was in the next cage waitin' for a circuit judge. He'd killed a deputy an' a posse caught up with him. The town woulda lynched him if they coulda got their hands on him.'

'So how come you took to ridin' with him?'

'The night we wuz in the jailhouse Morgan bust us out after killin' the sheriff,' Wilson said. 'That's what he

199

tol' us but we heard different since. Anyways, he tol' us the town would lynch us if we stayed in the jailhouse. So we rode with him.' He looked down at the floor. 'When we tried to quit he said he'd kill us first.' His eyes came up to meet Thornton's. 'We were jest too plumb scared to do anythin'.'

'So how have you quit now?' Hurley asked, speaking for the first time since entering the room.

'Afore he left he tol' us we were no good to him. Warned us if we went to the sheriff he'd know an' he'd a man here in town to take care of us.'

'Did you see this man?'

Reese shook his head. 'No, we reckon he was bluffin' but we were too scared to take a chance. Morgan did meet up with a passel of riders an' sent them on to Alveston. That's where he's heading for.'

Thornton's mouth twitched. 'Two of 'em ain't gonna make it. You got any idea where Morgan's gonna be holin' up?'

Reese shook his head. 'We woulda

200

bin plain dumb to ask him about that. But I did hear him say once that he had to see a feller who made arrows, and then he laughed but there was nothin' funny.'

Thornton stood up from his chair. 'You got more to say afore we go down to the sheriff's office?'

Glumly, both men shook their heads. Thornton looked at Hurley.

'What were you men planning to do?' Hurley asked.

'We're timber hands,' Reese said. 'We saw the mill boss here this mornin' an' got hired. We were gonna start tomorrow. We can do jobs in the mill he ain't got hands fer.'

Hurley slid his sidearm into its holster and raised his eyebrows in the direction of Thornton. 'What do you think?'

Thornton hiked his shoulders. 'What the hell.' He turned to the men. 'This is your lucky day. You mess up here an' I'm gonna come back an' kick both your butts. C'mon, Mr Hurley, Miss

Amanda can play her fiddle an' settle me down.'

Thornton and Hurley were finishing their breakfasts in the town's chop-house when Billy and Amanda came through the door. Amanda was the only woman present and several men shot admiring glances across at her. Thornton and Hurley got to their feet as Billy and Amanda reached their table.

'Billy and I are ready to leave,' she explained. Her fingers strayed to the top of her jacket. 'The livery man gave me a fair price for my brooch, and I've bought a horse.'

'What happened to the horse you were riding?'

'The livery owner knows the cousin of poor Mr Wilkins. He'll make sure the horse gets to him. It's only fair he should have it. I told him about the wagon and his son is taking a couple of horses and hopes to bring it back here.'

Thornton dug into a pocket in his pants and pulled out several gold coins. 'There's your money, Billy, an' there's twenty for seein' Miss Amanda safely to Cheyenne.'

Billy took the coins without counting them and thrust them into a deep pocket in his vest. 'Thanks, Mr Thornton. Any time you need a tracker you know where to find me.'

'I'm sure I'll see you both again,' Amanda said, looking at Thornton and Hurley. Thornton was aware that her gaze lingered on the Englishman.

'I'll be in Cheyenne late this year,' Hurley said promptly. 'I hope we can meet there.'

'I'll write you with my address,' Amanda said, her face pink.

With smiles and nods of farewell Billy and Amanda left them. Hurley turned back to Thornton and reached into a pocket. 'I owe you twenty dollars.'

Thornton smiled at the Englishman. 'Save them, Mr Hurley. You'll need them to buy back Miss Amanda's brooch.' He took his seat again. 'We'll finish up here and follow Morgan back to Alveston.'

# 11

Blue smoke from a thick cigar clouded the air above J. T. Walker's desk. The rancher glared in turn at Thornton and Hurley, who sat in front of the desk facing him.

'You're damned lucky I was over at the Lazy Y when you two rode in.' Walker bit hard on his cigar, his face blood-red with anger. 'What the hell have you two been doin'? Where's my gran'son? You two been ridin' 'round in damn circles this past week?' He stared hard at Thornton. 'Mr Hurley's a schoolmaster, but I'd heard you could handle yourself.'

'Mr Hurley's shootin' with his long gun saved my life,' Thornton said evenly. He knew there was little point in crossing swords with the rancher. Walker was worried about his grandson, and his anger was understandable.

'We have not been wastin' our time. We know William is still alive. Morgan has a woman with him now who knows nothing of Morgan takin' the boy. I don't know why that should be but I aim to find out.'

'An' how the hell you gonna do that? An' how does it help to get my gran'son back to me?'

'The more we learn, Mr Walker, the greater the chance of bringing William home safely,' Hurley said.

Clouds of smoke bloomed above the desk again as Walker sucked on his cigar. 'You think Morgan will kill him? Don't spare my damn feelings, Thornton. Tell me what you reckon.'

'There's a real chance he'll let him go if he gets the money. He must know you have the wealth to hire as many men as it takes to hunt him down. Otherwise, I reckon he'd have killed him by now,' Thornton said.

'An' you sure William's alive?'

'He was alive when Morgan left Willings Ferry to head back here. We

205

spoke with the clerk at the hotel in Willings Ferry, who saw them ride out of town.'

Walker took the cigar from his mouth, staring at the glowing end for a few seconds before placing it again between his lips. 'OK, I've been thinkin' hard. I'm gonna pay Morgan,' he said. 'My gran'son means more to me than a pile of yellow metal, an' I ain't gonna take chances with his life. I'm just waitin' for this sonovabitch Morgan to tell me where he wants the gold. I'll pay you for your time, Thornton. Hurley can make the delivery.'

'I reckon that would be a mistake, Mr Walker,' Thornton said.

'Don't tell me what to do!' Walker barked. 'You're a hired hand o' my son-in-law an' you do what I say!'

Thornton's face remained expression-less, seemingly unruffled by Walker's manner. 'S'posin' I tell you Morgan's got someone workin' for him in town, an' there's a chance he'll know where Morgan's holdin' William. Last time

Morgan was around he holed up in an old sheepman's shack. We can get to Morgan afore he's expectin' it.'

Walker looked at Hurley. 'You go along with that?'

'I've never had any cause to doubt what Mr Thornton says,' Hurley said carefully.

'Why the hell didn't you tell me about this afore?' Walker barked at Thornton.

'I hadn't known you were goin' to make a deal with Morgan.'

Walker tore the cigar from his mouth and hurled it into the spittoon by his desk. Thornton heard sizzling noises for a few moments. 'Fer Chris'sakes! Don't you understand? William is my gran'son, an' I want him back safe and sound.'

'Then this could be the way to do it,' Hurley said quietly.

There was silence in the room for a few moments. 'OK,' Walker said heavily. 'You got until Morgan tells us where he wants the gold. Then we do as he says an' pray we get William back.'

Thornton got to his feet. 'I'll let you know what I find in town.'

Thornton and Hurley left Walker staring ahead, seated motionless behind his desk. The two men went down the steps from the door of the house, Thornton heading for where his horse had been stabled overnight.

'Thanks fer backin' me in there.'

'I hope you know what you're doing,' Hurley said. 'I think you're right in saying that Morgan has a man in Alveston. But it could be anyone.'

'I'll be back in a few hours,' was all Thornton said.

\* \* \*

Thornton headed down Alveston's Main Street, his mount at the walk. If he had any hard riding ahead of him he'd need to change his horse. The barn at the Bar J had spare horses from their remuda so it shouldn't be difficult to borrow one for a few days. He knew that nothing could stop Morgan putting a bullet into William's head if that was what he decided to do. But Morgan was no fool. He'd know that with William dead, his own life would be short.

Thornton looked around. He needed to identify Morgan's man in the town and he had a notion how to start. The townsfolk were going about their business as normal. Outside the sheriff's office Landon was talking with an old-timer wearing a battered straw hat and bib coveralls. Landon raised a hand in greeting as he saw Thornton but then turned back to continue his conversation. Thornton passed the general store, mindful that he'd need more ammunition for his Colt and his Winchester.

He couldn't blame Walker for wishing to do all he could to get his grandson back alive. But as tough as he was, the old rancher was just that, a man who had spent his whole life thinking about cattle. Sure, in the early days he may have had trouble with the Indians, and there would have been the occasional shooting between drunken cowboys, but he knew little or nothing of men like Morgan, who would kill a fellow human being for a few cents' worth of whiskey.

Once he'd got his hands on the money, Morgan would surely quit the Territory as fast as he was able. There was the woman, too. Her being with Morgan puzzled him. Was she Morgan's woman or was he using her as part of his plan to extort money from Walker?

He turned his mount's head down the alleyway leading to the town's livery. When Morgan had been asked in Willings Ferry where he was going he'd said that he was going to see a man who made arrows. He'd first thought that Morgan was referring to Billy Three-Eyes, but a moment later he realized that it was a stupid notion. Then he'd remembered his first day in Alveston. Butler, the liveryman, had appeared in the barn clutching an arrow that he was making for the Shoshone who helped him with the horses.

Butler didn't square up to Thornton's notion of a man to be in cahoots with Morgan but he told himself he had to start somewhere, and the livery was as good a place as any. He stepped down from his saddle as he reached the opening into the horse barn. He didn't expect trouble he couldn't handle from Butler but instinctively his hand dropped to the butt of his Navy Colt and eased the sidearm in its holster. Then he walked into the barn.

'Butler! You around?'

Save for a rustling of straw as horses moved in response to his call there was silence in the barn. Then from behind one of the stalls a tall man, his complexion the colour of copper, in workpants and a woollen shirt, stepped into view.

'Mr Butler outta town,' the Shoshone said. 'Back two days.'

'OK, I'll see him then.'

Thornton turned on his heel and walked out of the barn. Dammit to hell! Had Butler ridden out with news for Morgan? It wouldn't have been difficult for him to learn that the men tracking Morgan had returned to the Bar J the previous night. When he and Hurley had arrived at the ranch they'd been seen by a dozen cowboys and the young fellow who looked after the horse barn. Maybe one of them had cause to visit the livery that morning.

As Thornton stepped up to his saddle he pondered his next move. Back to Walker or keep on trying? Would Morgan have gone into the saloon since he'd returned? It was unlikely but maybe he should check. Morgan would deliver his demands in the next day or so, telling Walker where he wanted the money. He knew that once Morgan's poke was full he'd disappear, and that meant he, Brad Thornton, had risked his life and worked most of the summer without earning a penny. He had no illusions about what would happen if he didn't catch up with Morgan. Whether William lived or died, Walker and Frewen would sweep him aside with a bunch of Pinkertons.

Thornton walked his mount along Main Street, stepped down to secure his horse at the rail and went up the steps to push through the batwing doors of the Silver Horse. The calico queens had finished cleaning up from the previous night and the place was deserted save for a short, bow-legged old-timer wiping down the bar counter and the older woman playing cards with a young woman whose name, Thornton recalled, was Rosie. He walked across to their table.

'You ladies care for a drink?' he said.

The older woman, name of Lottie, Thornton remembered, looked at him with her hard eyes. 'I ain't been called a lady since way back. I'll have a glass of wine, an' Rosie will have a sarsparilla.' She looked across at the bow-legged man. 'You hear that, Fred?'

'An' a beer for me,' said Thornton.

'Comin' up, mister.'

Thornton picked up a chair, spun it round and straddled it. 'You recall I was talkin' of a feller in a blue hat.'

'I remember,' Rosie said. 'But he ain't been in since we talked.'

'You said he could be out at the old sheepman's shack.'

'He ain't there now,' Lottie said. 'The sheepman's back with all his dirty animals.'

Thornton put down a coin on the table as the bow-legged man delivered the drinks. 'You ain't seen a feller in a blue hat, I s'pose?' He touched the top of his ear. 'Gotta slice off here.'

The bartender shook his head. 'I bin here every night for the last month. I ain't seen him.' He put the glasses down on the table and retreated to the bar.

Lottie picked up her wine and raised it in Thornton's direction. 'I hear you rode shotgun for the stage. Why's a smart feller like you doin' somethin' like that?'

Thornton shrugged. 'I owed Mr Jenkins a favour. The regular shotgun was sick.'

Lottie exchanged glances with Rosie. 'You talkin' 'bout Zeke Fletcher?'

Thornton thought for a moment, recalling his conversation with Warren Jenkins. 'Yeah, that's the feller.'

'He looked fine to me. Never misses his cards if he can help it.'

Thornton frowned. 'You sayin' he was in here on that night the stage left with me ridin' shotgun?'

'Sure he was. Played cards like he allus does. Reckon he musta left 'round midnight.'

Thornton took a long gulp of his beer. 'Is he in town?'

'He walked past here this mornin',' Rosie said, 'so I guess he is.'

'You know where I can find him?'

'Sure,' Lottie said. 'He's got a cabin an' a little barn back o' the billiards place.'

Thornton got to his feet. 'I'm mighty obliged to you ladies.'

'You gonna come an' see me some time?'

Thornton looked down. 'Yeah, I'll do that, Rosie. But I'm kinda busy now.'

He exchanged glances with Lottie,

who again raised her glass in a salute, a wry smile on her face. A few minutes later he tied his horse to the rail in front of the billiards parlour and walked down the alleyway to Fletcher's cabin.

A low fence, badly in need of a coat of paint, stood ten feet from the cabin door. Thornton pushed through the gate, which was short of a couple of nails on one of its bars, crossed the hardpack and knocked loudly on the door. A few moments passed and then Thornton heard footsteps approaching from behind the door. A tall man wearing woollen trousers and a blue shirt stood in the open doorway. His face was pale, save for the stain of a bruise on his cheek. His eyes were red-rimmed and he screwed them up against the sun over Thornton's shoulder.

'Zeke Fletcher?' Thornton asked.

'Sure, that's — ' He broke off, his eyes widening as the muzzle of Thornton's Navy was rammed against his chest.

'Back up, Fletcher. We're gonna have words.'

Fletcher did as he was told, backing into the room behind him, fear showing in his eyes, his face turning even paler. Thornton gestured with his free hand that Fletcher should sit in one of the two chairs at the side of the rough-hewn table. Staring at Thornton and the gun in his hand, Fletcher backed the couple of feet to the chair and slumped down, his head hung low.

'I'm gonna say two words,' Thornton said. 'You don't tell me all you know an' I'm gonna take my knife and start carvin' you up.' He paused. 'Bart Morgan,' he said.

Fletcher jerked his head up. 'Why you doin' this? I've done all that Morgan said.'

Thornton looked at him for a few seconds. 'An' what did Morgan tell you to do?'

'You know all about that! How I had to get the list of passengers on the stage and then go sick the last time the stage left town.'

'How much did he pay you?'

'Goddammit!' Fletcher exploded. 'He's your boss, ain't he? You know he didn't pay me a cent! He's fooled my woman into thinkin' he's not the sonovabitch who's tellin' me he'll send her back in pieces if I don't do as he says.'

Again, Thornton was silent for a few seconds. Then he looked around the cabin. A pot stood on a square stone by the fire that burned in the corner of the cabin. He lowered his sidearm and slid it back in its holster.

'You got coffee in that pot?'

Fletcher looked up at him, his expression showing that he thought Thornton was playing tricks with him. 'Yeah, I just made it.'

'I'll get the pot,' Thornton said. 'You rustle up a couple of mugs.'

For a moment, Fletcher didn't move. Then, as Thornton crossed to pick up the pot, he stood up and moved to a cupboard and took out two metal mugs. While he did this, his eyes never left Thornton, seemingly still doubtful about Thornton's intentions. He placed the mugs on the table and Thornton topped them up from the pot, before taking the seat on the opposite side of the table. Continuing to study Thornton, like a jackrabbit caught in a flare, Fletcher again took the other chair.

'I'm trackin' Bart Morgan,' Thornton said. 'You're gonna help me find him.'

'You a lawman or somethin'? If Mr Jenkins hears what I done he'll kick me loose.'

Thornton shook his head. 'I'll not tell him. I'm workin' for an Englishman over at Powder River.' He took a sip of his coffee. 'Tell me how you got tied up with Morgan.'

'He arrived in town a while back. Tol' me my wife was now his woman over at Willings Ferry.' Fletcher looked away from Thornton. 'I came back from the War unable to be a father agin. We was lucky. We had a fine son — he works out at the Bar J, an' she woulda stayed with me, I know that.' He pulled his lips back from his teeth in a gesture of regret. 'But I'd got a hankerin' after playin' cards durin' the War. I lost everythin' we had. It was too much for her. She moved to Willings an' now does sewin' an' stuff for the smart ladies over there. She thinks Morgan's a decent feller but he's usin' her so he can rob the stage.'

Thornton looked hard at Fletcher. 'Can you keep your mouth shut?'

Fletcher nodded. 'I reckon so.'

'The name William Frewen mean anythin' to you?'

Fletcher shook his head. 'No, I — ' He stopped abruptly. 'Hold on. I think his name was on the passenger list of the stage comin' south.' He frowned. 'But I think he's a boy.'

'The son of a wealthy Englishman,' Thornton said grimly. 'Morgan took him and he's holdin' him for ransom.'

Fletcher's jaw dropped. 'Fer Chris'sakes! That's why Morgan was here this mornin'.'

'Morgan was here? You damn sure? Morgan favours a blue hat, part of his ear's missin'.'

'Don't fret. I know Morgan. Sonov-abitch told me he'd kill my wife if I didn't do more of what he wanted.'

'What's he got you doin' now?'

'He's gonna send one of his men at dawn tomorrow carryin' a message for Mr J.T. Walker at the Bar J. I hevta deliver it. I asked him what was goin' on.'

Fletcher's fingers touched the bruise on his face. 'He knocked me down. Tol' me I didn't need to know an' I should think o' my wife.'

Thornton leaned back in his chair. He'd be wasting his time being here at dawn tomorrow. Morgan's messenger wouldn't talk, reckoning that Morgan would catch up with him no matter how long it took.

'How long you got to deliver the message?'

'Soon as the message arrives I gotta ride for the Bar J.'

Thornton stood up. 'I'll be at the Bar J waitin' for you.' He looked down at Fletcher. 'We'll get your wife back. She may not want to come home but at least you'll know she ain't in harm's way.'

Fletcher nodded, his face stiff. 'Tell her I'll never touch a deck o' cards agin.'

* * *

Thornton didn't spare his mount on his ride back to the Bar J and the animal was running with sweat and blowing heavily when Thornton reined in by the horse barn at the ranch. The young man who looked after the horses pulled up his mouth as he stepped forward to take off the saddle.

'Guess you're in a kinda hurry, Mr Thornton.'

Thornton slapped the horse's rump. 'He's up to it. No harm done. See he gets plenty o' feed. I'm gonna need him fresh first light tomorrow.'

'I'll see to it, sir.'

Thornton looked towards the Big House as Hurley came down the steps

222

to the hardpack. 'Did you discover anything?' he asked.

Thornton drew in breath. The Englishman had stood tall when they'd been bushwhacked on the trail to Willings Ferry. Hurley was a good man but if Morgan's demands reached Walker the Englishman would obey the rancher's orders like a good soldier. That meant Morgan would get the money, probably kill William and Fletcher's wife, and Hurley if he had the chance, and disappear.

'Nothing,' Thornton said, answering Hurley's question. 'I guess we'll have to wait for Morgan to show up.'

'It was worth a try,' Hurley said gloomily. 'I'll tell Mr Walker we should get the money ready.'

# 12

Thornton buttoned his woollen shirt, pulled on his pants and buckled his gunbelt before easing his Navy Colt into its holster. He put on his trail jacket, picked up his boots and carried them to the door. There was enough morning light to see the door latch and he eased it up slowly before stepping into the narrow corridor. For a few seconds he stood still, listening for signs of movement in the ranch house. Reassured by the silence, he closed the door behind him and headed for the stairs leading to the main door.

Taking care that the heavy door made as little noise as possible he pulled it shut behind him and bent to pull on his boots. Within twenty minutes the house would come alive and he was intent on being away by then. He crossed the hardpack to the horse barn, anticipating that his horse would be saddled as he'd ordered; but he was still surprised when a figure appeared in the doorway holding a lamp high to throw splashes of light on the young man's face.

'Howdy, Mr Thornton. I got your roan ready an' waitin'. I stuck a few biscuits in the saddle-bag an' I got coffee on the stove.'

'You've done fine, young feller,' Thornton said. 'I'm gonna take one o' those biscuits right now with the coffee.'

Ten minutes later, buoyed by the coffee and ready to face the day, he was walking the roan towards Alveston. By his reckoning he'd meet Fletcher away from the ranch and he'd be free to make his decision without hindrance from Walker or John Hurley. Could he justify following a plan that would lead to gambling with William's life?

When he'd reached a couple of miles from the ranch he reined in and slipped from the saddle. He looped the reins around a nearby cottonwood, allowing the horse to lower its head and nibble at the bunch and buffalo grass. A fallen tree trunk provided a convenient seat on which to wait and he pulled from beneath his shirt the small cotton bag hung around his neck on a cord. He took brown paper from his shirt pocket, a pinch of Bull Durham from the bag and rolled himself a smoke. He reckoned he didn't have long to wait.

But he was wrong. No rider appeared on the trail from the town. The minutes ticked by and the movement of the morning sun told Thornton he'd been waiting for over an hour. He stood up, freed the reins of the roan from around the cottonwood, and stepped up to the saddle. Turning the horse's head he took the trail to Alveston. Maybe the messenger hadn't arrived. Fletcher was unlikely to have ridden out to the Bar J empty-handed. Maybe Morgan had changed his plan. Thornton sucked air into his lungs. The only way to find out was to get hold of Fletcher.

The roan was a good mount, and it

wasn't too long before Thornton found himself breaking from the trail and taking to the hardpack of the town's Main Street. There'd been no sign of Fletcher, so Thornton headed for the far end of town.

He left his roan at the rail outside the billiards parlour and walked down the alleyway. The door to Fletcher's cabin was closed and he rapped loudly. There was no sound and nothing moved behind the door. After a few moments Thornton pushed at the door and stepped into the cabin. There was no sign of Fletcher. He crossed the cabin to peer behind a heavy cloth. Behind it was a bunk but it was empty, save for a rough grey blanket pushed back.

Maybe Fletcher was in the small barn out back, although he'd surely have heard anyone moving around his cabin. Thornton left, walked across to the barn and pushed open the door. The early morning sun shone through a gap in one of the walls. Thornton breathed in deeply. Light fell on the top half of

Fletcher's body in the dirt of the barn, his head twisted sideways, his sightless eyes appearing to stare towards Thornton, an outstretched arm seeming to point a finger.

Blood from the side of Fletcher's head had run down his shirt, staining the dirt. Thornton crossed to the body and dropped to one knee. That was when he saw the marks close to Fletcher's hand. Left to die he had managed to scrawl marks in the soil with a tobacco-stained finger.

For a couple of seconds Thornton was unable to identify the grooves in the soil. Taking care, he stretched out his hand, and with a forefinger followed the patterns made by Fletcher. The dying man, it appeared, had made a final effort to leave a message. Thornton could see written in the dirt the word 'BAJA'. Thornton knew French but Spanish was beyond him. Maybe Landon or someone back at the Bar J could help. Fletcher had said he'd try to discover where Morgan was holding William. Maybe he'd tried too hard. Thornton stood up and looked down at the body.

'You did fine at the end, Fletcher,' he said aloud.

★   ★   ★

Landon looked down at the letters he'd written on a scrap of paper on his desk. He pulled up his mouth, and shook his head. 'BAJA don't mean anything to me. Could be Spanish, I s'pose,' he said. He looked past Thornton to the cowboy who'd been in the office when Thornton called and who Thornton vaguely recognized as being from the Bar J. 'You know any Spanish, Pete?'

The cowboy shrugged. 'I knows a little. Lotsa Spanish talked when the beef comes up from Texas. 'Baja' means a sudden drop o' some sort. Like when a feller gets lynched.'

'Best we can do, Thornton,' Landon said. He looked at the cowboy. 'Pete, you mind steppin' out for a while? I gotta talk to Mr Thornton.'

'Sure, Sheriff. Anyways, I've finished here and I hevta get back to the ranch.'

When they were alone Landon handed Thornton the scrap of paper he'd written on. 'You gonna tell me what's goin' on?'

Thornton took a few minutes explaining how Fletcher had been connected with the taking of William Frewen. 'I reckon I got Fletcher killed,' he said, his expression grim. 'I'd pushed him into tryin' to find out where Morgan was holed up. Morgan's messenger mebbe suspected a trap an' killed him. Coulda bin Morgan himself.' He picked up his hat from the corner of Landon's desk. 'All we can do now is wait for Morgan to tell us where he wants the money. We're all gonna have to pray he lets the boy live.'

★  ★  ★

After a visit to the general store, where he bought ammunition, Thornton rode hard for the Bar J. Maybe while he'd been in town Morgan or one of his men had delivered the message to Walker now that Fletcher was no longer around.

Whenever the message arrived saying where the money was to be delivered he intended to argue against Hurley being used. The Englishman was a fine shot with a long gun and he was brave. But he was trained as a regular soldier and a poor match for a cunning no-good like Morgan. There'd be a problem if Morgan named someone to deliver the money, maybe J.T. Walker himself, but it was unlikely. Morgan's interest was in the money, not the man who delivered it.

An hour or so later he slowed the roan to a lope and then to a walk to cool down the animal as he approached the Bar J. There was no sign of activity around the Big House, although sounds of metal on metal came from the horse barn. The young man who had given him coffee and biscuits that morning was about his chores.

Thornton thought for a moment to turn his roan into the horse barn but decided to leave him at the rail close to the house where the animal could take water from the trough. He'd find out what was happening in the house before he had the horse fed, in case he needed to ride out immediately. After securing his horse he went up the steps to the house. He pushed open the heavy door to find Hurley standing only a few paces away from him.

'I heard you arrive,' Hurley said. 'Did you learn anything?'

'Plenty,' Thornton said. 'Is Mr Walker in the house?'

Hurley nodded. 'In his study.'

'OK, I'd better tell him what's going on.' He looked hard at the Englishman, and for the first time he used his given name. 'John, I found Morgan's man in town, but it ain't gonna help us none. I ain't givin' up but Morgan's got the whip to our backs.'

Hurley gave a quick nod, his face expressionless. 'I'll hear what you have to say to Mr Walker.'

A couple of minutes later both men were occupying the two chairs in front of Walker's desk where they'd sat the previous evening. Walker glared at Thornton.

'Where the hell you been this morning?'

'In town,' Thornton said. 'I went in to see the man Morgan's been usin'.'

The rancher frowned. 'Hold it there, Thornton. You tellin' me you had the time to find Morgan's man from all the townsfolk in Alveston an' be back here by noon?'

'I found him yesterday. Zeke Fletcher, whose place I took when I rode shotgun on the stage.'

The rancher's face turned puce. 'Why the hell didn't you tell me?'

'I wasn't sure Fletcher knew anythin'.'

Hurley jerked up in his chair as if he'd suddenly thought of something.

'My God! Fletcher! An old English word for a man who makes arrows!'

'What the hell you talkin' about, Mr Hurley?'

Hurley shook his head. 'Nothing important. Something we were told in Willings Ford.'

For a moment Walker looked as if he was about to bawl again at Hurley, then he breathed in deeply. 'OK, let that go.' He turned to Thornton. 'What did Fletcher tell you this mornin'?'

'He tol' me nothin'. I found him shot dead in his barn. But Fletcher did somethin' as he was dyin'. He took from the pocket in his shirt the scrap of paper Landon had given him and placed it on the desk. 'That word mean anythin' to you?'

Both men leaned forward to examine the paper.

'Spanish!' Walker said. 'Means something like a mountainside where there's a sudden drop.' He looked up at Thornton. 'Fer Chris'sakes! What's this got to do with findin' William?'

'When he was dying Fletcher scrawled that word in the dirt of the barn. I reckon he was tellin' me somethin'.'

'Why would he do that if he was one of Morgan's men?' Hurley asked.

'He wasn't. Morgan's got hold of Fletcher's wife an' was using her to force Fletcher to carry out his orders. I tol' him yesterday we'd save his wife if he could find out where Morgan was holed up.'

'You done your best, Thornton,' Walker said. 'I ain't denyin' it, but I want William back safe. That's all that counts.'

'I'm ready to deliver the money, Mr Walker,' Hurley said.

Thornton looked at him, his mind turning over how he could persuade both Walker and John Hurley to let him deliver the money himself. Before he had chance to speak there was a knock at the closed study door.

'Yes!' Walker called. 'Come on in.'

The door opened, and Thornton, turning in his seat, saw one of the house servants standing in the doorway. She was a short, fair-complexioned girl, maybe fourteen or fifteen years old. She gave a little bob, which surprised Thornton. Maybe she'd worked for an Englishman before.

'One of the hands is at the door, Mr Walker,' she said in a light voice. 'He says he has an important message for you.'

'Tell him to come in here, Emily,' Walker said. 'Leave the door open.'

'Yes, sir.' Again she gave a short bob and turned away and disappeared down the corridor.

'You think this is Morgan's message?' Walker said.

Before either Thornton or Hurley could reply a short, broad-shouldered man appeared in the doorway. He pulled off his battered hat and looked directly at Walker.

'The name's Fortune, Mr Walker. I ride with the remuda.'

'Sure you do, Henry. You're doin' a fine job. What you got for me?'

'I was in town seein' the blacksmith. This feller came up to me an' said he had to get a message to you as fast as he could. He gave me five dollars.'

Fortune reached beneath his shirt and pulled out a slim package and brought it into the room, handing it over to the rancher.

'What did this man look like, Henry?' Thornton asked.

'Looked like a pilgrim, sir. He was all dressed up in a city suit, and a black derby hat.' He hesitated for a moment before he touched the side of his head. 'He was missin' the top of his ear, looked like a knife cut or somethin'.'

Walker looked at both Hurley and Thornton in turn. 'OK, Henry. You've done well. Don't spend all those five dollars on Saturday night.'

Fortune grinned. 'Try not to, Mr Walker.' He nodded to the three, replaced his hat, touched the brim in the direction of the rancher and left the room, closing the door behind him.

Walker looked down at the package on his desk. 'I guess this is what we've been waiting for,' he said heavily. He began to tear the outside cover.

'If Morgan was in town this morning it means he has at least one other man with him, probably more,' Thornton said. 'We were told at Willings that he'd met up with some riders. Now that Fletcher's dead he needn't keep up the pretence with the woman, so he'll have left someone to guard her and William.'

'You reckon Morgan'll kill her?'

Morgan would probably kill both her and William, thought Thornton, but it would be no help to put it into words. He looked at Walker. 'What does Morgan want?'

Walker appeared to read through the message twice before replying. 'He wants the money delivered to Mallet's Ford. The money is to be carried by one man only, driving a buggy pulled by a single horse. If other riders are seen the boy will be killed. If any weapon is carried or hidden in the buggy the driver will be killed. The buggy is to arrive at the ford at exactly noon tomorrow.' Walker looked up. 'I know the ford across the river. It's about twenty miles south of here.'

'This sounds like a plan he's worked out. He's done this before,' Thornton said.

'I'm ready to deliver the money,' Hurley said.

Walker nodded. 'William will feel better knowing you're there.' He stood up from behind the desk. 'We'll have the buggy ready first light tomorrow. I'll hand you the money just before you leave.' He led the way out of the study. ''Bout time we got somethin' to eat.'

The three men walked along the short corridor at the end of which stood the maid, who had brought the news of Fortune waiting to deliver a message.

'Mr Thornton,' she said. 'The feller from the horse barn wants to see you. He's waitin' on the porch.'

Thornton turned to the other two men. 'I'll join you shortly.'

He went out to the porch where the young man who'd provided the coffee and biscuits that morning stood waiting. 'Mr Thornton, can I have a word?'

'Sure. I'm listenin'.'

'You goin' after my pa's killer?'

Thornton frowned. 'Now hold it, there, young feller. What's all this about?'

'You never asked me my name but it's Harry Fletcher. Pete Sheen was in the sheriff's office this mornin'. He told me you'd found my pa dead in his barn.'

Thornton nodded slowly, remembering Fletcher had told him about his son working out at the Bar J. 'Yeah, I am goin' after your pa's killer but I got some other business to clear up first.'

'When you go chasin' him can I ride with you?'

Thornton hesitated. 'You an' your pa close?'

Harry shrugged. 'Not really, I guess. The War did fer him, I reckon. I ain't seen him for a year or more.'

'How about your ma?'

Harry shook his head. 'Ain't seen her for a while. She's over in Willing doin' sewin' and stuff.' He stared hard at Thornton. 'I ain't got brothers, so it's down to me to go after Pa's killer. An' I can shoot. Ask folks in town, I bin winnin' shootin' competitions for the last three years.'

'Your pa's killer is not a man to chase on your own,' Thornton said. 'You're not gonna do your ma any favours you get yourself killed. I'll make a deal with you. When I ride outta here you'll get a chance to ride with me.'

Harry appeared to think over Thornton's offer. Then he nodded. 'OK, Mr Thornton; makes sense, I reckon.' He touched a finger to his hat. 'G'night, sir.'

For a few moments Thornton watched the young man walking across the hard-pack in the direction of the bunkhouse. He'd have to find a way of leaving without him. The young man meant well but there was a heap of difference between shooting at a target and shooting at a man, especially when the no-good was trying to gun you down. He turned on his heel and went back into the house. He was ready for some grub.

The ladies had already finished their supper and left the room when he walked back to where Walker and Hurley were seated at the table. One of the maids must have been waiting for Thornton. As he took his seat she appeared alongside him and placed a plate before him. Thornton looked down at the large beefsteak and picked up his knife to cut the meat into smaller pieces.

'We were just talking about William,' Hurley said. 'Mr Frewen is keen that he doesn't stay away from England too long. He has in mind a political career for the boy and reckons it's important he knows the country well.'

You're talking as if William was up in his room asleep, Thornton thought. Unless Morgan kept his end of the bargain when the money was handed over there'd be no life in politics for the boy. He'd have no life at all.

Walker jabbed a fork into a piece of his steak. 'The boy'd be better off in Wyoming,' he said. 'Runnin' cattle's a fine life an' there's money to be made. We'll be a state soon and Cheyenne could give William all the politics he needs.'

'It's true William is interested in ranching,' Hurley said. 'Every place we stopped he'd badger me to ride with him to the nearest herd of beef.'

Thornton grinned. 'Over at Powder River I heard him takin' on his pa an' rode with him to the brandin' — ' He stopped suddenly and swung around to Hurley. 'What did you say then?'

Hurley looked puzzled. 'I said how keen William was on seeing cattle.'

Thornton shook his head vigorously. 'No! Your exact words.'

'I said William would badger me. That means — '

'I know what it means,' Thornton cut in. He pulled out the scrap of paper and placed it on the table. 'Look at that! The stage driver tol' me that Fletcher could hardly read or write. 'Baja' isn't Spanish. That's Fletcher tryin' to write 'badger'.' He turned to the rancher.

'Any place hereabouts by that name?'

'There's Badger's Drive about fifty miles to the east,' Walker said.

Thornton shook his head. 'Too far,' he said.

'I can't think — ' Walker broke off as if recalling something. 'There's Badger's Creek about ten miles south of here. But the settlement's been abandoned for two or three years. Nobody lives there now.'

Thornton looked at the other two, a grim smile appearing on his face. 'Gentlemen,' he said. 'I reckon we've just found William.'

# 13

As dawn was breaking the Big House of the Bar J was silent save for the low voices of the three men who sat around Walker's desk, mugs of strong black coffee in their hands. An hour before, Walker had ordered Henry Fortune to ride out and keep watch for strangers. Since then Thornton, Walker and Hurley had been weighing up their next move. Suggestions were made, only to be discarded and other notions considered. They all agreed that the wording of Morgan's demands showed that he knew what he was about. They could not afford to make mistakes.

'Morgan is thinkin' you'll try to catch up with him at Mallet's Ford,' Thornton said to the rancher. 'He's trying to convince you that he'll carry out his threat to kill William. He can't know we've worked out where he's holed up. Our best chance is to hit him early at Badger's Creek.'

'S'posin' we got it wrong an' Morgan's not in Badger's Creek?'

'Then we ride to Mallet's Ford an' do exactly what Morgan wants.'

'OK. You thinkin' of a posse for Badger's Creek? There's not much time.'

Thornton shook his head. 'That'll stampede Morgan. Mr Hurley has said he'll ride with me.'

Walker pushed back in his chair. 'Just the two of you? Are you crazy?'

'There'll be men with Morgan, but I'll wager they know nothing about the money he's demandin'. Come a showdown I reckon they'll not stand.'

'We're both trained soldiers, Mr Walker,' Hurley pointed out, 'and we'll have the advantage of surprise.'

'We shall need a buggy with us or there'll not be time to meet up with Morgan at Mallet Ford if we have to,' Thornton said.

'I'll drive the buggy,' the rancher said promptly.

'No, sir,' Thornton said firmly. 'The Bar J rests on your shoulders an' lots of families depend on you. There's gonna be shootin' an' we ain't gonna take chances with your life.'

Before Walker could reply there was a knock at the study door.

'Come,' called Walker.

The door opened. Henry Fortune stood at the door. 'There's a rider coming up the trail from town, Mr Walker.'

Thornton stood up. 'OK, Mr Hurley and I will handle this.' He looked across the room at the gun case pinned to the wall. 'You got an eight-gauge among that iron?'

'Sure, you take it,' Walker said.

'Let's go take a look, Mr Hurley.'

In the light of the dawn Thornton with Hurley alongside him could see the outline of the rider as he trotted his mount in the direction of the Big House. Thornton took one of the cartridges he'd removed from inside the gun case and loaded the scattergun. Then he took up his position at the foot of the steps from the porch, the scattergun held in the crook of his arm. The rider drew closer and for the first time Thornton was able to see his face. He unloaded the scattergun.

'What brings you out here, Billy Three-Eyes?' Thornton called. 'You're s'posed to be in Cheyenne.'

'Me an' Miss Amanda rode half a day, an' then she took the railroad. Said I should come back to my wife and boys.'

'I thought she had no money.'

'Yeah, well, you know that money Mr Hurley gave me . . . ?'

Both Thornton and Hurley laughed aloud. 'She's smart, I guess,' Thornton said. 'Anyways, what brings you out here?'

'Got a message for you from Sheriff Landon. Says he ain't too keen on you shootin' Morgan down on Main Street.'

Thornton smiled grimly, standing back a pace as Billy stepped down from his saddle. 'We reckon Morgan's at Badger's Creek. Out there Landon's just another cowboy with a gun. Not that I couldn't do with him along,' he added.

'Yeah, I guessed that when Landon tol' me about Fletcher.' Billy touched the butt of his sidearm, looking at the Englishman. 'You ridin' with us, Mr Hurley?'

'What's this with 'us', Billy?' Thornton said. 'I thought you'd put gunfightin' behind you.'

The tracker hiked his shoulders. 'That lovely woman o' mine said she didn't marry me cos I sat at home when a child's life was in danger. An' I ain't here to be paid.'

Thornton looked at Hurley, who gave a short nod. 'A good man to have along,' he said.

'OK, Billy. Mr Hurley will show you where to get coffee. I'm gonna have a word with young Fletcher.'

He crossed the hardpack as Hurley and Billy went up the steps and entered the Big House. Harry Fletcher was giving water to a big grey halfway along the line of stalls when Thornton entered the barn. He looked up as Thornton approached.

'Howdy, Mr Thornton. What can I do fer you?'

'You drive a single-horse buggy?'

'Sure I can.'

Thornton held up the scattergun. 'You ever use one o' these?'

'Been on plenty o' turkey shoots, Mr Thornton.'

'OK. Have the buggy ready to go when I tell you. Henry Fortune's down the trail a mite; tell him to take over here.' He stared hard at the young man. 'We're gonna ride after the man who killed your pa. You can carry a sidearm with the scattergun. But listen hard. You do as I say at all times. You're drivin' the buggy we need to have with us. Nothin' more.'

Fletcher nodded vigorously. 'I've got it, Mr Thornton.'

For a second Thornton considered telling Harry his mother was with Morgan but then decided it would only faze the young man. If the woman was killed, better Harry knew about it afterwards.

An hour later the three men astride their horses, and Harry, seated on the bench of the buggy, were assembled in front of the Big House. On the porch looking down at them Walker stood, with his wife alongside him. She was holding his arm tightly.

Thornton touched a finger to the brim of his Stetson. 'We're gonna bring back your gran'son, Mr Walker.'

The rancher, his face grim, said nothing, giving only a brief nod. His wife stepped forward a pace. 'May God go with you all,' she said, her voice quavering.

Thornton touched his Stetson again and turned his horse's head. 'Move off, Harry. Keep the pony at the trot. We'll fall in behind you.'

With a flick of the reins above the pony's head, Harry set the buggy rolling. Thornton touched his heels to his mount and the other two men took up position each side of him.

'Keepin' this pace we can reach Badger's Creek in plenty o' time if the buggy has to go to Mallet Ford,' said Billy, who had been briefed by Thornton on what was happening.

'How close can we get to the settlement?' Hurley asked.

'We're gonna come on it from the high ground to the east, but there's maybe five hundred yards of open ground before the first shack.'

'Unless Morgan's got sloppy he's gonna have long guns looking over that ground,' Hurley said.

'There's a stand of cottonwoods over on the north side of the settlement. We work our way around there an' we stand a chance o' gettin' among the cabins without them seein' us.'

'What sort of shape is Badger's Creek in?' Thornton asked.

'Pretty good. The folks who built there were handy with tools an' most of the cabins an' stuff are still standin'.'

'Why did they leave?' Hurley asked,

leaning forward in his saddle to look past Thornton at Billy.

'Cholera. Back then folks thought it was caused by somethin' in the air. Feller who was leadin' the pilgrims had the house burned where two men had died and ordered everyone into their wagons.' Billy shrugged. 'I guess folks are still a mite scared. Cholera's killed a lot o' folks in the Territory an' settlements are still learnin' to look after their water supply. Anyways, nobody's been back.'

'Morgan either hasn't heard that or he's smart enough to know what brings the cholera,' Thornton said. 'I was in a town once where they had cholera. It ain't pretty.' As if to chase away his bad memories he called out, 'OK, Harry, we can go faster.'

★ ★ ★

The mid-morning sun warmed Thornton's back as he touched the sides of his horse with his spurs and pulled out to lead the buggy and the two others towards the rim of the high land east of Badger's Creek. Two hundred yards from the beginning of the slope leading to the settlement he held up a hand. Harry slowed the buggy to a halt and Hurley and Billy reined in to bring their horses to a halt. Thornton stepped down from his saddle and pulled his Winchester from its scabbard.

'OK, let's go see what we've got,' he said. 'If we're gonna make those cottonwoods Billy talked about we'll haveta come up on them from the north. Harry, stay here an' keep hold of the horses. Don't tie 'em.'

'Sure thing, Mr Thornton.'

The three men, crouching to avoid being outlined against the sky, ran forward to the edge of the high ground, throwing themselves to the ground to lie flat out. The morning sun was beginning to shine on the cluster of cabins sited two hundred yards before the riverbank. Stretching in the direction of the river a rough street, overgrown with buffalo grass, separated the cabins. Tracks were scuffed through the grass where men and horses had crossed from one line of cabins to the other. The only sign of habitation was a string of horses strung along a rail halfway down the street.

'Nine horses,' said Thornton, his voice kept low. 'Say three for Morgan, the boy and the Fletcher woman.'

'We're outnumbered two to one,' said Hurley soberly.

'It's gonna be tough,' Billy agreed.

'Remember, they ain't soldiers with Morgan — ' Thornton broke off as he saw something move beyond the nearest cabin to the river. After a moment a group of men appeared.

'Morgan's there!' Hurley exclaimed. 'I think I see his blue Stetson. My God! There's William!'

Hurley was right, Thornton realized. Among the group of men Thornton saw the broad-shouldered figure of Morgan holding the boy firmly by his arm. William was putting up resistance, dragging his feet but helpless in Morgan's grip.

'Where's the woman?' Billy asked.

As he spoke two more men appeared from around the corner of the last cabin, one man gripping a woman by her upper arm. The woman had to be Harry's mother. Thornton took a quick backward glance to check that Harry had stayed by the buggy as ordered. Satisfied, he made his decision.

'We ain't gonna chance a shot,' Thornton said. 'We could hit William or the woman.'

'Those men are most likely saloon-trash,' Hurley said. 'But how do we know some of them haven't been threatened by Morgan like the two timbermen back at Willings Ferry?'

As the Englishman spoke a faint cry reached the three men. In the middle of the rough street Harry's mother had pulled away from her captor and was running down the street, her short steps hampered by her ankle-length dress. A loud cheer rang out from the group of men.

'Go get her, Texas,' came a shout

from one of the men.

With a loud whoop one of the men broke from the group and chased the woman down the street. Catching up with her, he threw his arms around her waist and hoisted her across his shoulder. Kicking and screaming she was carried back to the group, to the raucous cheers of the others.

'Guess that answers your question,' Thornton said heavily.

The three men continued to watch as the group, now led by Morgan, divided in the centre of the street. Morgan, still holding on to William, entered one of the cabins on the left. The others, surrounding the still kicking and screaming Mrs Fletcher, began to enter a cabin over to the right.

'I'm gonna kill every one o' those bastards,' Billy said, his voice rasping.

Noise exploded a few feet from Thornton's ear. An instant later he realized that Hurley had fired his Winchester. As he watched the men by the cabin he saw the last in line clutch at his chest and fall to the hardpack. There was a moment when the men stood still, staring in the direction of Thornton and the two others. Then, with loud shouts, they ran for their horses.

'The woman . . . ' Hurley said tersely.

'For Chris'sakes, Hurley! You tryin' to get William killed?' Anxiously, Thornton looked towards the cabin that Morgan and William had entered. The door remained closed. Surely Morgan had heard the shots and the ensuing loud shouting?

Billy ratcheted his Winchester. 'Here they come! There's gonna be shootin'!'

'Hold your fire,' Thornton ordered.

The air buzzed with slugs above their heads and all three men levered their Winchesters. Thornton took out his Navy and placed it on the ground beside him. As the three men prepared for the onslaught they saw the line of advancing riders split as they galloped towards the top of the rise. The riders appeared bent on a cavalry charge, rifles in their raised hands, legs held fast against the sides of their mounts. Two of the men held their reins in their teeth, long guns at their shoulders.

'Hell! They look as they know what they're doin',' Billy muttered.

'Billy left, Hurley right,' Thornton rapped out, aiming at the centre of the line. He guessed the range at four hundred yards.

'Fire!'

Three Winchesters were fired simultaneously. Thornton saw a rider flung from his saddle as a horse fell to its knees. The rider hit the ground head first and lay still. Another rider was jerked from his saddle as his mount continued its run towards the rim of the high ground. The line of men broke, veering to the right and racing down the slope away from the cluster of cabins, making for the trail alongside the river.

Thornton swore under his breath. A slug had hit the ground only a foot or so from where he lay, and dirt had sprayed over the side of his face. He brushed it off with a hand which shook slightly.

'You two OK?' Thornton asked.

Both men nodded, sweat running down their faces. 'Those bastards had done that before,' Billy said. He looked across at the riders now some distance away. 'You reckon they'll come back?'

'They'll think about it.'

'William,' Hurley said flatly. 'That's why we're here.'

'You two stay up here with the buggy,' Thornton said. 'That makes three of you if they come back. I'm goin' down to get William.' He held up his hand as Hurley opened his mouth to speak. 'No, John. You're a fine soldier and mighty handy with a long gun. That pack o' no-goods come ridin' back you're gonna be needed up here.'

Hurley pulled up his lips in a gesture of regret, and then nodded.

They rolled away from the rim, getting to their feet only when they were hidden from Morgan spotting them, and retraced their steps to the horses. Harry sat in the buggy, the scattergun across his knees, holding on to the reins of the three horses. Each of the men took his reins and prepared to mount.

'I saw what happened,' he said excitedly. 'You chased 'em off with fine shootin'.'

'They could come back,' Thornton said grimly. 'If they do, you're gonna be firin' that scattergun o' yourn. Mr Hurley an' Billy's gonna be with you. I'm gonna go down an' get William an' the man who killed your pa.'

'You be on your guard, Mr Thornton.'

Thornton turned to the other two. 'If William's alive so far there's a chance that Morgan will still let him live if he gets the money.' He leaned into the buggy and picked up the leather bag at Harry's feet.

'Get William back,' Hurley said, 'and you could let Morgan ride out of here.'

Thornton looked at the Englishman for a second. 'Yeah, I could do that.'

* * *

Twenty yards from the first pair of cabins Thornton kept his eyes fixed on where he'd caught his last sight of Morgan and the boy. Why hadn't Morgan appeared at the sound of shots? Had he calculated that a posse had found where he was holed up? Maybe he'd decided his best chance of escape was to hold the boy his prisoner, threatening to kill him. He'd know that a powerful man like Walker could override any decision made by the local sheriff. Anyways, Badger Creek was outside Landon's jurisdiction, and Morgan would know that. He'd also know that the nearest marshal was based many miles away.

Thornton clutched the leather bag containing the money firmly in his hand and dug his heels into the side of his horse. By the time he reached level with the first cabin he was bent low over the animal's neck. The thought crossed his mind that if what he was planning to do went wrong he could easily break a leg and Morgan would be able to shoot him down like a dog.

He kicked his feet from his stirrups and as his horse reached the cabin opposite to where Morgan was last seen he rolled from his saddle, hitting the ground hard and rolling towards the cabin where he reckoned the woman was to be found. His back muscles were twitching with the thought of slugs from Morgan's gun and his feet and hands scrabbled through the rough grass before he threw himself through the door and into the cabin. His Colt, already in his hand, was aimed at the shadowy corners with a sweep of his outstretched arm.

'Don't you touch me!'

There, seated on the dirt floor, her back against the wall of the cabin, her knees pulled up to her chin, the tear-stained white face of Mrs Fletcher stared up at him.

'It's OK, ma'am.' Thornton sucked in air, his chest heaving. 'William's gran'pa sent me.'

'You're tryin' to trick me!'

'No, ma'am. I'm here for William, nothin' else,' he said, climbing to his feet.

Her expression relaxed a little. 'That poor boy . . . '

'I've other men with me,' Thornton said. 'We'll soon have you safe.'

No sooner were the words out of his mouth than he heard the sharp crack of fire from long guns and the deep crump of a scattergun being fired. Morgan's men had returned and now Hurley and the others were fighting back. Thornton strained his ears for the sounds of approaching riders indicating that Morgan's men had gained victory. But the seconds ticked past and there was nothing save for the light breeze rustling through the nearby trees. Hurley and the others had played their part.

William's life now depended on him.

He edged his way to the door and opened it an inch to look across to the cabin where Morgan, he assumed, was still holding William. Nothing showed. He opened the door an inch or so more.

'Fer Chris'sakes!'

Wood splinters flew above his head as the sound of the shot reached him. He pushed the door almost shut, leaving only a narrow gap. The shot had come from over to his right. Morgan, he realized, had managed to switch cabins. If the slug had been a foot to his left he'd have been on the ground, a hole in his head.

'Morgan! You hear me?'

There was a pause, then, 'I hear ya!'

'Your men have ridden out an' you're on your own. My men will be here soon. I've got the money. Let the boy go, an' you can ride out.'

'You're a goddamned liar. I ain't trustin' you!'

'All Walker wants is his gran'son back safe. The money means nothin' to him.'

Pulling back his arm and opening the door wider he hurled the leather bag into the middle of the street. It landed among the tall strands of buffalo grass, the gold coins rattling against each other.

'You want the money, Morgan? There it is!'

Thornton pulled the door almost shut, but again leaving a gap wide enough to peer across at the cabins. Nothing moved. The only sound in the air came from birds close to the river. What was Morgan waiting for? And why had there been no sound from William? Was he with Morgan? Had Morgan killed him before shifting to another cabin?

'William! Can you hear me?'

The seconds ticked past. Just when Thornton was beginning to think that maybe Morgan had already killed the boy, he heard a quavering voice coming from the cabin where Morgan had first entered.

'Yes, I c-can hear you.'

Thornton knew the boy must be terrified but he pursed his lips, blowing out air with relief. William was alive and maybe Hurley was right. Free the boy and Morgan could ride out. The loss of the money wouldn't hurt Walker. He wanted his grandson safe. Frewen would put his son's life far above any notion of Morgan facing justice. Maybe he'd be mindful of not having to pay if Morgan hadn't been brought to justice within three months. That was the deal. But to hell with any deal, Thornton decided. A boy's life was more important than a handful of gold coins.

'Morgan! I give you my range word,' he called. 'Take the money and ride outta here.'

He waited for an answer, more curses maybe, but there was no reply. Had Morgan somehow managed to get back into the cabin holding William?

'William! Stay steadfast. We'll soon have you home.'

'Yes, Mr Thornton.'

Christ! William had recognized his voice. He cursed himself for not anticipating William would call out his name. Had Morgan caught what the boy had said? Did he know the name of the man who had killed one of his brothers and delivered his brother Charlie to jail? In the next moment he got his answer.

Morgan let out a bellow of rage. One after another, six slugs smashed into the door, forcing Thornton to duck behind the stout timbers of the cabin, his back hard against them. In the corner of the cabin Mrs Fletcher, her eyes bulging, threw back her head and screamed with fear.

'Thornton, you murderin' bastard! You shot down my brother an' I'm gonna kill you for it! Then I'm gonna kill the boy an' take the money! You gotta woman an' I'm gonna go after her!'

Morgan's raging response gave Thornton his chance. He threw open the door, his Colt held high, firing rapidly in the direction of Morgan's voice, not caring if he hit his target, content to keep Morgan's head down. The long strands of buffalo grass felt like grasping tentacles around his boots as he charged towards the cabin where William was being held. Bracing his shoulder, he hit the door like a ramrod and tumbled into the cabin. A terrified scream came from the boy.

'It's OK, William! It's OK!'

Thornton gasped. He snatched reloads from his belt and swung around on his heel, sliding the slugs into his Colt while a couple of paces from the door. Then the solid timber hit him in the face. Christ! He was sent staggering, struggling to keep his balance, but then fell on his back in the corner of the cabin. His Colt flew from his grasp, spinning away to land somewhere near the boy. Morgan towered above him, his pistol held high. Below the blue Stetson Morgan's eyes burned with hatred; veins protruded from his flesh by his misshapen ear. His lips were pulled back.

'You're gonna die like the dog you are!' Morgan spat out the words.

Then he must have seen from the corner of his eye William scrabbling towards Thornton's Colt, for he shifted his gaze. He brought his pistol around to aim at the boy, who was on his hands and knees, his eyes bulging with fear, his outstretched hand reaching for Thornton's Colt where it lay by the rusting pot-bellied stove.

'An' I'll kill the whelp first!'

Thornton scrabbled at his boot-top. 'Morgan!' he bellowed.

Momentarily, Morgan took his eye off the boy to look down.

Thornton pulled the trigger of his pocket pistol twice, the .32 slugs hitting Morgan between the eyes. For a moment Morgan stood quite still, his mouth agape as if he was unable to comprehend the turn of events; then blood spurted from his head as his lifeless body crashed to the floor like a tall pine felled in the forest.

# 14

The final sweet notes of the violin faded away. For a moment the open hall of the Bar J ranch was silent and then a great cheer erupted, ladies clapping furiously, men cheering. Pink-faced with pleasure, Amanda lowered her violin from her shoulder and curtseyed to the men and women before her.

J.T. Walker got to his feet. 'Miss Amanda, that's the finest music ever heard at the Bar J. The new orchestra in Cheyenne is mighty lucky to have you and we all thank you for taking the time to visit Alveston.'

The rancher held up a hand for quiet as again cheers sounded around the hall. He turned to the assembled men and women. 'This is a happy day for all of us. We again welcome to the Bar J Mr Moreton Frewen and our daughter Maude, Mr Thornton and Mr Hurley, whose brave efforts have meant that William, our gran'son, is safe again with us. Over these past four weeks, William has been able to recover from his ordeal.' He glanced at Moreton Frewen and smiled. 'And has been able to see what ranchin' is all about.'

Thornton exchanged glances with Hurley as William, seated between them, wriggled on his chair with embarrassment, his face red. 'Pa will be put out if Grandpa goes on about ranching,' William whispered.

Walker looked directly at William. 'We'll take another look at the beef tomorrow, William, I promise. OK, folks,' he added, 'Mr Thornton will shortly be taking Miss Jordan into town to meet the new schoolmarm from the stage an' when they return we'll have supper.'

The dozen ranch-hands who had stood at the back of the hall while Amanda entertained them moved to help the maids rearrange the chairs, leaving the remaining men and women to break into small, friendly groups around the hall. Moreton Frewen joined Thornton and Hurley, placing his hand on William's shoulder.

'I trust, Hurley, you'll not bring William back to England after a year chewing tobacco and drinking hard liquor!'

Hurley smiled. 'No, sir, I think not! We have a good plan of study for the year, and Miss Amanda will be teaching him the pleasures of fine music.'

'I wish you good fortune in your forthcoming marriage to Miss Amanda. I know William will be in good hands for a year.' Frewen turned to Thornton. 'And what are your plans, Mr Thornton?'

'Miss Jordan and I are going East.' Thornton hiked his shoulders. 'Somebody once told me that no man can be a gunfighter for ever, an' I guess my luck is due to run out. Anyways, the Reverend wishes to return to Boston and his family.' He glanced at the four-glass mantel clock that stood on the shelf above the open fireplace. 'Now you must excuse me, Miss Hetty is determined to meet the new schoolmarm from the stage.'

He moved away from the group as Hetty Jordan, smiling, crossed the room to join him. 'The buggy's at the door. We'll be in time to meet the stage,' he said.

She took his arm and together they made their way across the room, exchanging a few words with J.T. Walker and promising to return as soon as possible. At the door Thornton paused before reaching up to the hook for his gunbelt.

Hetty Jordan smiled, seeing his hesitation. 'You promised no more guns,' she said.

He grinned, buckling his belt. 'Just until we take the train to Cheyenne. I'd feel undressed without it.'

Outside, in the late afternoon air, Thornton breathed in deeply. As pleasant as it had been listening to Amanda's music he realized he had some adjusting to do before he'd be content to sit on a soft chair for several hours making polite conversation as he once did as a much younger man. But he knew his decision to quit his way of life was the right one. The government was bringing real law to the West and soon there'd be no place for men like him. He had no wish to be a town sheriff, throwing drunken cowboys out of saloons. A few years ago he'd considered applying for a marshal's position but then decided he couldn't stomach the politicking. Then he burst out laughing as he looked in the direction of the trail to Alveston.

'Cowboy's in a hurry,' he said, pointing to the galloping horse, heading towards them. 'I guess he was hopin' to hear Miss Amanda's music.'

They stood on the porch watching the rider break from the trail to the hardpack surrounding the Big House. Then Thornton's smile faded as he saw the rider rein in his horse and step down from his saddle, allowing the horse to walk free.

'Go back in the house, Hetty,' Thornton ordered. 'Don't look at the rider.'

'But — '

'Do as I say!' Thornton barked. 'Do it now!'

Hetty's face turned pink at Thornton's tone, but she turned on her heel and stepped back through the open door. Thornton's fingers briefly touched the butt of his Navy Colt as he moved down the steps to the hardpack. Some fifteen yards away the rider stopped, his eyes never leaving Thornton.

'Hell! I reckoned I was gonna haveta kill some folks afore I got to you, Thornton! You sure are makin' it easy for me!'

'How'd you break out, Charlie? They're gonna hang you for sure.'

Morgan let out a harsh laugh. 'They're gonna haveta catch me first!'

'I heard you killed the liveryman at Coyote Bend.'

'Yeah, tough little bastard, that German. He took a long time to die, but he told me your name in the end.'

From behind Thornton a voice rang out from the porch. 'I've got a

Winchester on him, Brad!'

Without taking his eyes off Morgan, Thornton called out, 'Put it down, John. Hermann was a good man, an' Morgan's gonna answer to me for what he did.'

Morgan glanced up at Hurley for an instant. 'Never killed an Englishman afore,' he sneered. 'They bleed like us?'

'Make your move, Morgan,' Thornton said, his teeth clenched.

Morgan's hand was hovering above the butt of his pistol. There was no fear in his eyes, only hate. 'You killed my brothers, goddamn you! Now it's your turn.'

Two shots rang out across the hardpack. For an instant both men stood straight. Then, as Thornton watched, Morgan crumpled, blood gushing from the wound between his eyes. His lifeless body fell face-down on to the ground.

Only then, his Colt raised, did Thornton move forward to turn Morgan over with his boot. He stared down. He'd been aiming for the man's heart.

Another six inches higher and Morgan would have shot him down.

With a flick of his hand he tossed his Navy Colt away into the dirt. One hand went to his waist and he unbuckled his gunbelt, allowing it to slide to the dirt. He stood quite still as Hetty ran past Hurley down the steps and towards him, her arms outstretched.

## THE END

We do hope that you have enjoyed reading this large print book.

Did you know that all of our titles are available for purchase?

We publish a wide range of high quality large print books including:
**Romances, Mysteries, Classics**
**General Fiction**
**Non Fiction and Westerns**

Special interest titles available in large print are:
**The Little Oxford Dictionary**
**Music Book, Song Book**
**Hymn Book, Service Book**

Also available from us courtesy of Oxford University Press:
**Young Readers' Dictionary**
**(large print edition)**
**Young Readers' Thesaurus**
**(large print edition)**

For further information or a free brochure, please contact us at:
**Ulverscroft Large Print Books Ltd.,**
**The Green, Bradgate Road, Anstey,**
**Leicester, LE7 7FU, England.**
**Tel:** (00 44) **0116 236 4325**
**Fax:** (00 44) **0116 234 0205**

*Other titles in the*
*Linford Western Library:*

## DARROW'S GAMBLE

### Gillian F. Taylor

'Set a thief to catch a thief!' It's a risky strategy for a lawman to take, but Sheriff Darrow has very personal reasons for wanting to catch bank robber Tom Croucher. Forced to stay in Wyoming, Darrow is relying on two convicted criminals, Tomcat Billy and Irish, to do the job for him. But Tomcat hates Darrow, while Irish wants to go straight. They join Croucher's gang, but who deserves their loyalty — the outlaw or the sheriff?

# DALTON AND THE SUNDOWN KID

## Ed Law

When Dalton rides into Lonetree looking for work, he finds a town crippled by the local outlaw — the Sundown Kid. Tasked with resolving the Kid's latest kidnapping, Dalton must deliver a ransom to the bandit to secure the safe return of young Sera. Culver. However, before he reaches the rendezvous point, the ransom is stolen. Then a fearsome shootout leaves him stranded in the wilderness . . . With the fate of a woman at stake, can Dalton fight the good fight and prevail?

# THE AFTERLIFE OF SLIM McCORD

## Jack Martin

Rogues Blackman and Tanner have seen it all, but nothing has prepared them for what they find in the town of Possum Creek: the preserved corpse of their long-ago compadre, the outlaw Slim McCord, being exhibited in a travelling carny show! Outraged, the pair decide to steal him away and give his mortal remains a decent burial. But before he is laid to rest, Slim will take part in one last bank job alongside his old friends . . .